I0764607

Ruby
Coral
Carnelian

by

Mary Borsellino

Omnium Gatherum
Los Angeles

Ruby Coral Carnelian

ISBN-13: 978-0615790862
ISBN-10: 0615790860

First Edition

For Maria, who read fairy tales to me when I was small,
and typed in all the spells in King's Quest III.

Del is twelve when the Ruby Warlock remarries. This new wife has twin children, a boy and a girl, aged ten. Del can tell from the first that this new wife has never wanted to be a mother and has never quite learned the trick of pretending. That doesn't mean that she's a bad person, or deliberately malicious. Just that the role she's been handed by life doesn't suit her.

A part of Del wonders if he's supposed to find this observation tragic. In his experience life almost never provides people with the things they need, let alone keeps away the things they might not want. As far as burdens go, Nicholas and Kelsie are almost certainly at the better end of the spectrum.

The twins have hair in a deep honey-gold shade, wavy and thick. If they care one way or the other that their mother doesn't want them, Del has never seen them give any indication of it. Most of their time is spent at boarding school, and for Del the pair of them appear and disappear with the end-of-term holidays and are rarely mentioned in-between, at least not by their mother or the Ruby Warlock. Del thinks about them a lot, but that's just inside his own brain. There isn't anyone he could talk about them with while they're gone. During the months when they're away, Del sometimes slips into the unattended bedrooms left behind. The furniture and trinkets are all as still and undisturbed as an abandoned dollhouse, waiting for two perfectly-made china dolls to reappear and breathe life into the air.

Del, despite being older, is shorter than Nicholas and of a height with Kelsie. His skin is paler than theirs and lacks the scatter of tiny freckles which they wear across their noses and the delicate skin beneath their eyes. Del's skin is more like the blue-white of the skimmed milk that the kitchen cat drinks.

Del has been with the Ruby Warlock since before he can remember. He has to call him 'Master', or 'sir.' While spellcasting, Del has to call the Ruby Warlock by his name, which is Addanc. Names are powerful things, in spells. In Del's head, he is simply 'the Ruby Warlock.'

Sometimes the Ruby Warlock tells people that Del is his bastard child. Other times, he says that Del is a foundling taken in out of charity. On rare occasions, often occurring when an important visitor is in earshot, the Ruby Warlock even claims to have been married to Del's mother and that the three of them were very happy together, for a little while.

Del does not know how much or how little of it is true. All he knows is this: he is an apprentice always, a drudge sometimes, and a son never.

He doesn't mind not being a son. Nicholas has a hard enough time of it, and his mother only mothers him out of obligation. Being a son appears to involve, at the absolute minimum, a lot of questions about being warm enough, and about doing well at lessons, and keeping collars and cuffs clean of ink stains. Far easier, Del thinks, to be an apprentice. Del's real name is Rowan, but he's called that so rarely that he would have to pause and think before answering to it. His hair is straight as pins and falls in sooty locks across his forehead, darkest black-brown save for one thick streak of ashy grey above his right temple where the texture shifts from slippery-fine to coarse as wire.

Del doesn't remember what caused the change but assumes it was some spell gone wrong that has since faded into the general blur of burns and scratches and torn fingernails that preparing ingredients and reagents has strewn across his past.

Kelsie and Nicholas claim to be jealous of Del's life as an apprentice and plead with their mother to let them stay back from their boarding schools to learn at the Ruby Warlock's side instead. Their mother— who doesn't like Del, or indeed even think of him very much at all, since she treats the Ruby Warlock's professional life as something well beyond the scope of her own comfortable world— simply smiles and laughs and shakes her head, claiming to be amused at the wildly fanciful ideas her children dream up.

They might as well have begged to become pirates or gods or candle-flames, for all the serious consideration she gives their pleas.

In those early years, the three children— if Del can be said to be a child in the same way that Nicholas and Kelsie are children— have a surprisingly uncomplicated, easy-going camaraderie. The twins spend a sufficient amount of the year apart from one another that they are pleased, rather than antagonised, by each other's company during their holiday breaks. Del's quieter demeanour doesn't trouble them and neither does the fact that they have to teach him the rules to all their card games all over again every holiday, the knowledge having been pushed out of his head by incantations and recipes and other difficult things since the last time he saw them.

Nicholas and Kelsie are, to him, something not entirely unlike the black-furred kitchen cat; a friendly and occasionally demanding distraction that makes him smile and provides amusement. But the children who sometimes live upstairs are so different from Del that he never even considers the possibility of being truly close to them.

In many ways, he thinks to himself, he's got more in common with the cat.

For the most part, life after the Ruby Warlock's new marriage is not so different for Del from the life before.

Today is his seventeenth birthday and he gets out of bed, shivering in the autumnal chill before the dawn. His small, sparse bedroom is in the cellar of the house. For the most part Del likes that— it's comforting to think of the warm dark earth on all sides, kept at bay by nothing but the thin walls of wood and brick. But when the weather starts to turn cold, the little room feels like a dark pocket of ice, a place for storing nightmares.

There are some plants that are best plucked as the sun rises, so Del pulls on his boots and climbs the staircase up and out to the garden beds behind the kitchen. When he was very young, that flight of steps seemed to stretch up forever, but now he is almost grown up and the stairs have diminished down to a less impressive size by comparison. His little room isn't the deep-buried sanctuary he used to imagine it as, a place so far down that nothing from the harsh ordinary world could follow him.

Nowadays, Del understands that there's nothing but a lack of curiosity keeping the Ruby Warlock from descending down into the cellar. It's not a safe place. It never was. There's no such thing.

The dew has frozen into a thin frost on the plants, and Del's hands sting as they're mottled white and blue and pink from the cold. He can't wear gloves for this task— any potency gained from the dawn picking would be lost without the touch of skin to keep the delicate energies in balance.

Today, he knows, is the day when he'll have to decide what he wants to do about his situation. One way or another, something has to change.

He is an excellent apprentice. He prepares ingredients meticulously; he labels and sorts and cleans the work benches in the laboratory; he can titrate or distill a potion to perfection. He can kill a chicken for its entrails and wishbones and feet and then prepare the remaining carcass for a meal, wasting nothing.

His lessons and skills make him the perfect attendant, but are not the makings of an eventual spellcaster in his own right. That has never been the Ruby Warlock's aim;

Del has been brought up to be a helper, not a student who will one day gain mastery.

But he is a better learner than the Ruby Warlock planned for. His eyes are quick, his brain quicker. He has a sharp intelligence that absorbs more lessons than intended. And now, seventeen years old today, Del knows he's gotten *too* good. Very soon the Ruby Warlock will notice that the child in the cellar is very nearly a man grown, and therefore a threat.

He is too good at spellcasting, and too clever at borrowing the Ruby Warlock's wand and knife and brazier when nobody's looking. Very soon he is going to have to decide whether he wants to kill the Ruby Warlock or to run away.

Del's weighed each option, considered the pros and cons on either pathway, but is still torn by indecision. A small, childish part of him is reluctant to admit that the choice must be made at all. If that little part of him had its way, he'd live down in the cellar forever, getting up to pick icy leaves at dawn until the end of time.

Life has taught Del to be pragmatic, though, and so with a sigh, he carries the new plant cuttings into the kitchen and puts on the kettle to boil. Today he'll make a choice. Today he'll decide.

He fixes breakfast for the Ruby Warlock and the Ruby Warlock's wife, makes the day's bread, and gives the kitchen cat some milk in its bowl. It purrs and butts its head against his ankles. Del leans down to give the animal a fond pat on its head.

There's a quiet tap against the frame of the door out to the garden, which Del left open to let some fresh air into the cramped little room. He straightens up from petting the cat and turns. He's surprised to see one of the village girls that Kelsie is friends with standing there.

"You're Kelsie's step-brother, aren't you?" she asks with a small smile. "We don't see you in town much."

Del shrugs. He's never thought of himself as being

step-brother to the twins; that would imply that any of the family considered him to be a part of it.

"Kelsie posted me this. Said to give it to you," the girl goes on. Instead of holding out the letter in one gloved hand, she holds out the other hand for him to shake. "I'm Alicia."

He shakes her hand perfunctorily, but when he tries to pull away she squeezes his fingers for a moment and gives him another smile. "I work at the butcher's shop. You should come down the hill and say hello sometime."

She hands him the note and turns to leave.

Del leans against the door frame and watches her as she picks her way between the rows of plants in the garden. He can tell when somebody is flirting with him, even if it doesn't happen particularly often. He doesn't leave the house and its grounds enough for it to happen often. Alicia was definitely flirting with him.

It isn't that she isn't pretty or friendly— she's both— it's just that Del has never been interested in anybody, not like that. He feels very old and very tired inside his skin, and romance and love and flirting have always seemed like things which have nothing to do with him.

There are a lot of things in the world that other people have which have nothing to do with him. If he loses this apprenticeship, he's not sure there'll be anything much else left that's his at all, except for magic.

Before he has a chance to open the letter from Kelsie, one of the bells from upstairs rings. One chore leads into another, and hours pass before he gets a minute to himself again. His hands are sooty from topping up the fireplaces (the day hasn't grown any warmer than it was at sunrise, and the house is large and drafty, so there are a lot of fireplaces for Del to contend with), so he heads back downstairs to wash his hands at the kitchen pump before handling the envelope.

As Del passes by the Ruby Warlock's upstairs study, he hears muffled voices from inside and stops to eavesdrop.

Nobody's ever bothered to teach him that it's not well-mannered to listen in on other people's conversations. Even if they had he wouldn't care. Del spends too much of his life afraid of genuine dangers to bother getting worried about whether he's being properly polite or not.

He can tell, by the wavering echo that lingers after each word and sentence, that the Ruby Warlock is talking to somebody via the obsidian scrying bowl that's always kept polished to a perfect reflective shine.

"—you truly no longer want him. Name your price. I've been meaning to invest in another live specimen. There's a limit to how much substituting a familiar can accomplish. I haven't been able to set up anymore trapdoors in the city since the last child got used up. Do you imagine how trying it is to only have one point of access to a metropolis? Most inconvenient."

Del knows that voice; it belongs to a magician that the Ruby Warlock has known for years— the Coral Sorcerer, an even more powerful spellcaster than Del's extremely adept owner. Del has never liked the man. Even by the indifferent standards by which he judges all the magical adults he's met there's something in the way that he looks at Del that has always felt... appraising.

Now, that creeping feeling Del has always had on the back of his neck in the Coral Sorcerer's presence makes complete sense. He truly was being evaluated, judged for his suitability as a future spell ingredient.

Del feels a little sick and desperately hopes he's misunderstanding the conversation.

"Careful," the Ruby Warlock warns. "He's more powerful than you might expect. That's why I'm keen to be rid of him."

All right, so it seems he wasn't misunderstanding, then. Del barely dares to breathe.

The voice echoes and ripples from the scrying bowl.

The Coral Sorcerer laughs.

"There are easy charms to block the magics of a child,

Addanc. Don't fret on that account."

The Ruby Warlock doesn't respond immediately.

Del wants to believe that this is because the Ruby Warlock is hesitating. That he's having second thoughts about selling off the boy he sometimes claims as his own son.

It's a hard lie for Del to tell himself, though. He knows it's far more likely that the Ruby Warlock is pausing to consider how much money he can make.

"You can come collect him in the morning," the Ruby Warlock says. Del moves away from the door as quickly and quietly as he's able. Down the stairs and back into the kitchen, the cat is lazing in a sunbeam, washing itself as if there isn't a single thing wrong in all the world. Del goes over to the sink, works the water pump a few times and scrubs his hands clean with harsh soap. The gritty texture against his skin is rough enough to wake him up a little, enough that his eyes begin to sting and he has to blink several times to clear his vision.

Despite Del's pragmatism in the frozen garden just a few hours earlier, his certainty then about the need to run away, there's still a sharp cold thread of pain in his heart. He feels angry at himself as he dries his eyes. It's so stupid to get upset when he's got things to do that have to be done as quickly as possible.

He feels as if he can't properly get his footing on the stairs as he climbs down into his cellar.

A leather drawstring pouch that used to hold a set of runes is more than sturdy enough to withstand a spell to make the inside bigger than the outside, so Del casts it twice and shoves all his spare clothes and some of his bedding as well into the space created.

Then he adds in some of the harder-to-get reagents that he might need for potions or spells. Del's glad that most of the supplies for the Ruby Warlock's work are kept in the room where his apprentice sleeps. It would be too difficult and dangerous to risk a trip to anywhere else in the house on the way to making an escape.

Del's bag contains an extra shirt and pants, a waterproof cloak, some spare socks and underclothes, a screw-top jar of beetle wings, a stoppered flask of powdered snakeskin, and a small silk purse full of shards of wood from an old Ouija board.

He has very little money saved up, but doesn't dare go hunting through the house in search of more. Every second counts, as there's no telling when the Ruby Warlock will appear to prepare Del for collection in the morning.

Tying the leather bag to his belt, Del climbs up the stairs out of his cellar for the last time. He doesn't stop for a nostalgic last look. In a way, maybe leaving like this— with no time to plan or wallow in emotions— is better. It makes him concentrate on what's important.

Del cuts through the garden beds and out into the fields beyond, moving as quickly as he can from cover to cover. When he's a few miles away, he stops to get his bearings. It's only then that he remembers that Kelsie's letter is still in his pocket.

Her handwriting is all loops and flourishes, which is a nice change from the boxy, angular calligraphy that most spell books and tomes are written in.

Del

Since this letter is being delivered to you directly, I don't have to speak in code or mince my words. Nicky is in trouble. I hate that the three of us are so far away from one another for so much of the time. The most sensible course of action is for us to run away. Come to my school as soon as you're able & we will set out to help and collect Nicky.

If unable to assist please send reply informing of such.

xK

Her words make Del smile. Perhaps he has a little luck on his side after all. This might be exactly what he needs: a game of running-away played by children who have no true danger in their lives.

A day or two of indulging Kelsie— Del highly doubts it'll ever get far enough to involve Nicholas as well— will make it easier to run away in earnest when the time comes. It will make the whole transition feel less abrupt, more lighthearted.

The night is very dark once he's past the periphery of the illumination from the house's windows, and Del's grateful for that small mercy. Every moment that his escape goes undetected is another step toward freedom.

Kelsie's school is a two days' ride away. Del decides that flying is his best option, but that he should wait until morning to attempt going such a distance in a form he isn't used to.

In the meantime, he pauses for long enough to find a fairly straight and sturdy branch in the underbrush. Fresh wands aren't as reliable as broken-in ones, but any wand is better than none at all.

He turns himself into a girl and then back again, trying to keep his walking pace as even and rapid as possible through the transformations so that he doesn't lose too much momentum to the exercise. Twice, and then a third time, he shifts back and forth between form and gender. When he's confident that the wand will manage a full swap, he turns himself into a girl and stays that way.

When the sun comes up, Del steps out into the open and transforms into a crow. It feels good to fly and to give his aching legs a rest. As long as he can avoid being shot down by poachers, the rest of the journey to the school should be easy enough to accomplish.

Del's never seen a school before, except in illustrations. It looks impressive; something like a hospital and something like a house and something completely different all at once. There are a lot of girls in matching pinafores and straw hats and shiny shoes walking around in the midday sunshine when he gets there.

He spots a small laundry shed set on the edge of the grounds and a bit of distance away from any of the small strolling cliques. There's a washtub with a scrubbing board and a drying-mangle set outside the little walled room. Several long lines of wet clothes are hung up on cords strung between one side of the laundry and a series of sturdy posts planted a distance away.

Del swoops down low— not too fast, in case anybody should notice a swift-diving crow and decide to investigate— and flies through the unglassed open square in the wall of the laundry building which serves as its window.

After looking around to be certain that nobody can see him, Del shifts back to human form. The instant he does so, his nose begins to bleed.

Magic often has that effect on him when he pushes the limit of his powers. Flying that far without pausing is one of the biggest strains he's ever attempted, let alone accomplished, so it's no surprise that blood drips steadily off his chin and into his cupped hands as he remembers how to stand steady on human feet.

The bloody nose doesn't hurt particularly, but it does make his head throb, and there won't be any point to getting dressed until he can staunch the mess.

Del closes his eyes and takes a deep breath, drawing in the invisible filaments of life and energy in the world around him, the delicate auras around people and animals and grass and in the heavy motes of late pollen floating in the sunshine. The weather here is much more comfortable against Del's skin than the icier temperatures of home had been.

No. Not home. Nowhere is home, now.

When the nosebleed finally stops, Del washes his face in the sink and looks out the window. Several white pinafore aprons and dark under-dresses and woollen stockings are pegged to the lines beside the laundry room. They sway in the breeze as much as their heavy weight allows in the light wind.

Del frowns. He'd hoped there would be hats, too. His own shoes are nondescript enough that they'll suffice, but he doesn't have anything like the dark blue felt winter hat, or even the jaunty straw summer hat, that most of the girls wear.

"Nothing for it," he mutters to himself under his breath, wincing and closing his eyes. Growing hair isn't an especially exhausting little spell, but it feels incredibly peculiar as the change takes place. It makes an uncomfortable shudder run up Del's back. By the time he's done his hair is past his shoulder blades, a fine brittle fall of black with the single colourless lock on one temple.

With a hat, he might have passed for a girl even without changing his form— Del's chin when he's a boy is almost as sharp-angled as it is when he's a girl, his nose is about the same either way, and his lashes are always pale and long regardless.

In the age-spotted little mirror above the laundry sink, Del looks as pretty as any legitimate student at the school could hope to. Del makes his face smile at the reflection as he tucks that one pale streak of hair behind his ear. Perfect.

The clothes he steals from the washing line smell pleasantly of lemon and soap. Del dries the dampness from them absentmindedly as he makes his way back into the little laundry room, then curses his thoughtlessness as he has to deal with another nosebleed.

The clothes are well-made; more complicated than the simple working shirts and breeches he wears at... that he's used to wearing. After wrestling with the lace collar and the turned heels of the stockings for a little while, Del manages to get everything settled. His leather pouch fits neatly into the pocket of the dress, and he sets out to find Kelsie.

The way her expression lights up when she sees him makes it clear that Kelsie has recognised him despite the disguise. Without even bothering to bid farewell to the friends she's walking with, she breaks off from the small group and runs to him, grabbing him tight in hug that knocks the breath out of him with its strength.

"You came!" Kelsie exclaims still hugging him. Del can't remember the last time they embraced— it has probably been close to a year, or maybe even longer. Perhaps his current form of a girl removes some of the awkwardness that has crept into their friendship ever since their childhoods drew to a close.

She has the soap-sunshine-lemons smell to her too, from her own uniform, but beneath that Del catches the scent of her on his inhale. It reminds him of strawberries and smoke, though maybe it's nothing like either of those things at all and he only thinks of them because whenever he smells those things he thinks of her. On warm summer nights when she and Nicholas were home from school, the candles Kelsie kept in her room to read by were scented like strawberries. The smoke would cling to her come morning, caught in the thick waves of her hair.

Early morning and just-before-bedtime were the moments Del could most easily steal for himself; the Ruby Warlock would be busy with the business of being a good and dutiful husband to his wife. Del and Kelsie and Nicholas would climb trees then, or play cards, or chase each other up and down between the rows of vegetable patches.

It seems unfair, somehow, that Kelsie should smell the same now as she did then, as if nothing much has changed in the time since.

"I came," he agrees.

"Let's go to my dormitory where we can talk properly. The other girls will be out here for ages." She takes his hand, half-leading and half-dragging him towards the school buildings.

The room Kelsie shares with eleven other girls reminds Del in some indefinable way of his cellar. The curious similarity between the two places puts him more at ease, and so he stands still and submits to Kelsie's delighted examination of his girl-form disguise.

"It's wonderful! Can you make me a boy?"

"If you want," Del replies. "I'll probably have to if we're going to Nicholas's school. We'll get spotted straight away if we try to creep around as girls."

The mention of her brother makes Kelsie's expression darken. "Yes. I suppose I should pack some clothes for the journey, shouldn't I?"

"Collect whatever money you've got, too," Del says. "I didn't have a chance to look for any at the house before I left, beyond what I already had saved up under my own mattress."

Kelsie looks up at Del at that, her hands stilled on the brass handles of her chest of drawers. She looks touched, like he's said something kind, and after a moment he realises the misunderstanding. Kelsie obviously thinks that he immediately rushed off to be at her side— she's got no way of knowing that he'd already run away for his own reasons and that her letter was pure coincidence.

Del decides to let the misunderstanding remain as it is. It's nice to be thought of with admiration, even if it's not deserved.

"I'll need a coat," Kelsie murmurs to herself as she shoves clothing into a canvas satchel. "It's colder where Nicky is." She glances at Del. "You will too. If you don't have one, my old one should fit you since your arms and shoulders are smaller than mine."

"What's prompted all this, anyway?" Del feels obligated

to enter into the spirit of Kelsie's adventure as much as possible, now that he's gone and accidentally made her think that he's taken her letter seriously. He doesn't want his last memory of her to be of her hurt feelings at him.

And it wouldn't be so bad to see Nicholas one last time if they end up going to his school after all.

"I'll show you the letter," Kelsie says, and pulls a torn-open envelope out of the front pocket of the half-filled satchel.

Del reads over the short message and shrugs. "It looks normal enough to me."

Kelsie frowns, shaking her head a little. "What are you talking about? It doesn't sound like him at all! I wasn't even a sentence in before I knew something must be very wrong."

"Maybe he's distracted. School life seems pretty full of things to distract someone."

"No." Kelsie takes the letter back, scanning her eyes over the scrawled paragraphs of handwriting. "I can tell. I can tell something's bad."

"There might be another ex—"

"No!" The word cuts him off like a knife in the air. "I'm certain."

She sounds it, too. Del wonders what that's like, to know and trust someone so completely that you can be certain of something about them. It must be nice. Even when the certainty is bad. Even then, it must be nice.

"All right. We'll go as soon as everyone's gone to bed tonight," Del agrees.

Mollified, Kelsie nods. "Okay. Come on, you can wait in the old infirmary room upstairs. Nobody will go in there. I'll bring you up something for dinner a bit later."

She leads him up to a room which smells, paradoxically, like stale antiseptic and dusty soap. There are two teenager-sized stretchers fitted out with thin mattresses. When Del sits down on one it feels hard and unforgiving even to his healthy flesh. He thinks it's probably a very miserable thing, to get sick while away at school.

Too anxious to relax properly, Del spends his time contemplating where he'll eventually try to end up, when this distraction with the twins is over. Maybe he can find an out-of-the-way farm somewhere, one that needs somebody to work in the kitchen and the garden. They might appreciate somebody who can do a bit of household magic here and there. They might never get sick of him or want to sell him off when he gets to be too much trouble.

When Kelsie brings him something to eat, it's on a tray containing a large-ish china plate with a domed silver cover on top of it.

"Here, I brought you dinner," she says. "It's just the same as what we all got in the hall, sorry. Lamb chops with mint sauce and carrots and peas on the side. Oh, and I stole you one of the little trifles that were for dessert, but it got a bit of mint sauce spilled on it, so it might taste a bit off now. Cider to drink."

"How on earth did you get any of that?" Del asks before he recovers from his shock sufficiently to add "And thank you, obviously."

"I asked for it, of course," Kelsie replies, putting the plate down on a chair and removing the lid. She pushes the makeshift dining table over to where Del sits on the edge of the stretcher.

Del stares at her, puzzled. "Didn't anybody want to know what you needed all that spare food for? Or where you were taking it?"

"If you look like you know why you're doing something, most people don't ask what your reason is," she tells him. "That's half of how most criminals get away with things, I think. They just make it so nobody thinks to stop and check that they're supposed to do what they're doing."

Del nods. "Yes, that sounds about right." Despite his hunger, he's yet to touch knife or fork to the plate of food before him. The vegetables are brightly-hued and heaped high and the meat smells so good that Del's mouth is watering a little. "And the other half of how criminals get away with things is that they make ordinary people think that they're smarter than the criminals. That's how confidence men— con men, they call themselves— work. They make you think you're much cleverer than them, and so people will keep on getting sucked deeper into the scheme because they can't bear to admit that they've been had."

"Sounds like it's ego that's the trouble, either way," muses Kelsie. "But anyway, enough talking; your food will get cold if we chatter on."

"Mm," Del replies, noncommittal, but since there seems no way to put it off any longer without being impolite he cuts a small piece of lamb, adds mint sauce to it, and puts it in his mouth. It's delicious. He isn't sure why that makes him feel so guilty.

"I like your locket," Del says, attempting to distract himself from the strange feelings that the gift of food is giving him.

Kelsie smiles a little, touching the glass-fronted pendant at her throat. "Thanks. I always keep it in the drawer near my bed when I'm here at school or in my music box when I'm home at summer. Even though I never wear it, I... I didn't want to leave it here. I thought that, well, if I'm determined to take it with me, then I might as well wear it.

"It's a mourning locket," she goes on. "Some great-aunt of father's left it to me in her will."

Kelsie's tone is chatty but Del has known her long enough to be able to tell when something is of genuine importance to her. This locket is more than just a trinket.

"It had a lock of my father's hair in it when I got it, but I don't remember him so I don't miss him like I'm supposed to," she goes on. "So Nicky and I replaced it with a bit of Nicky's hair instead."

She blinks her eyes closed for a few long, quiet seconds. "We need to help him. No matter what. I need to help him."

This is a Kelsie very different from the one Del knew when they were children. It isn't just that she's growing up or that they've begun to move away from the closeness they had in younger years. There's a deep, slow sadness in her pretty mismatched eyes— one blue, one green, both long-lashed and large in her small face— and it makes Del wonder if he ever really knew her at all before now.

"I'll be back soon," she says as she leaves again.

The time passes more quickly, now that he's got a stomach full of warm food, and it's not long at all before the school has gone mostly dark and mostly quiet all around the little hospital room.

When Kelsie returns, dressed for travel and with firm resolve on her features, Del pushes the infirmary's window open as wide as it will go, and whistles softly out into the night air.

"Do you have any handkerchiefs spare?" he asks her as he waits. She rummages in the satchel slung at her hip, pulling out a small stack of them. Handing one over to Del, Kelsie puts the rest of them in back her bag. Del approves. They're useful things to have around. He keeps his in his hand.

A few minutes later a bat alights on the sill of the window. It looks up at Del with its ugly little bat-face and bright, curious eyes.

"This is going to sting a little," Del warns, and shrinks himself and Kelsie down to thimble-size. His nose begins to bleed, and he jams the handkerchief up against his nostrils to stop the flow.

"Eugh. You might have warned me. I'd've given you one of the old ones."

"What did you think I'd want a hanky for, except for something horrible coming out of my nose?" Del asks, his voice a bit muffled by the hanky in question. "That what they're *for*."

Kelsie shrugs helplessly. "I don't know! I thought you might be making a magic carpet or a hot air balloon or something out of it. You didn't say anything about blood or bats!"

"A hot air balloon?" Del repeats scathingly. Or, at least,

it would be scathing if it didn't come out sounding like 'a hod air balloo?' He rolls his eyes and follows Kelsie as she clambers up onto the bat's back and settles in, looking as confident as someone who sat on giant flying rodents every night of the week.

Since his nose is already a mess, Del casts a quick harnessing spell to keep them from falling off mid-air and then chirrups to the bat. With an answering trill, it flaps its wings and flies up into the huge blackness of the sky.

Kelsie's composure vanishes completely once they're in the air. Her delighted, thrilled laugh is just the same as Del remembers from when she was ten years old and he turned her paper kite into a dragon for the first time.

For a while, they just enjoy the strange joy of the experience, the gargantuan scope of the starlit world spread out below them as they fly. Eventually even that spectacle's not enough to keep the two of them enraptured, though, and so they sit facing one another on the bat's soft furred back, and start chatting again.

"When we moved from the prep grades into the higher school, we all had our magic levels tested. I did quite well," Kelsie tells Del. "But you know what Mother's like. She wouldn't hear a word of it, not for me. If Nicky had shown any talent for it, I'm sure he'd have been allowed to go on to study it, but he's completely hopeless. He can't even dowse."

Del's earliest memories are of dowsing. He'd been barely old enough to walk, his legs unsteady under him on those first tries. Divining for water and metal buried underground with a forked stick has long been used as a roughshod way of testing if someone has any natural magical propensity because even children can demonstrate the skill successfully if they have the talent for it.

It had always seemed like a grand game, toddling around the garden beds in search of the coins and thimbles that the Ruby Warlock had buried for him to find.

Del gives a few hard blinks to clear his vision, hoping

Kelsie hasn't noticed the memory's effect on him. Her attention is on the rushing scenery below them, though, and Del feels relief at that.

"So thanks to my ever-so-vigilant mother," Kelsie goes on, and for the first time Del catches an edge of bitterness in Kelsie's voice. "All I've really done is play with sparklers at parties, and that kite you enchanted for me when we were young. I've always wanted to give it a proper try."

"We've got time now, if you like," Del says.

"What could we do up there, though?"

He grins. "This." He waves his hand and swaps their eyes, leaving her with his light, light silver-blue ones and him with her one-blue one-green ones. Kelsie leans in to inspect the changed colour of Del's irises.

"Ha! If Mother knew magic could get rid of the parts of my face she thinks are ugly, she probably wouldn't be against me using it at all," Kelsie notes wryly. "She'd probably insist I keep them like this forever, whether I wanted them or not."

"I can swap them back, if you want."

"No, let's leave them like this. Just for now. See how long it takes Nicky to notice."

When they finally reach Nicholas's school, deep in the darkest part of the night, Del teaches Kelsie the trick of sneaking into the laundry rooms to find a suitable disguise.

"All right, now make me a boy," she says, as soon as they've cobbled together enough of a costume for each of them and abandoned their pinafores and under-dresses.

Del transforms Kelsie first. She pulls a lock of her hair forward and frowns at it, confused.

"I've still got long hair."

"Yes?" Del answers, confused by the statement. With a wince— his nose is already starting to bleed and it's about to get much worse— he closes his eyes and casts the same transformation on himself. "Why wouldn't we?"

"Because we're boys now. You got long hair when you made yourself a girl."

Del shakes his head. "I grew that separately. Hair length's got nothing to do, physically, with whether you're a boy or a girl."

"Oh." Kelsie screws her mouth up to one side, thinking. "We'll have to tuck it under caps. It'll look a little strange, but I'm not cutting my hair off just for a rescue mission, even if I *can* just grow it back later with magic. I worked hard at this hair."

So they dig out two caps from the laundry's extensive array of random clothing, and hide their long hair underneath.

"How are we going to find out where he is?" Del asks.

Kelsie gives him an odd look. "I know which dormitory he's in, of course. Not everybody is as bad at replying to letters as you are."

Del follows her, puzzled. Yes, Kelsie's sent letters home to him from time to time over the years, friendly little notes about what she's studying and how the weather's been. He'd always assumed they must be for writing exercises in class. He'd never even considered the idea of sending something back in reply— what was there in his life that someone such as Kelsie would possibly be interested in hearing about?

They creep along the halls to the dormitory. The handle of the door squeaks as Kelsie opens it, and they both wince at the sound as it pierces the stillness

By the faint moonlight through the room's large windows, they can see that one of the beds is empty and stripped of its bedding.

"See, I told you there was trouble," Kelsie hisses at Del. "He's been moved."

They close the door again— careful not to let the handle squeak— and stand in the hallway, at a loss for where to go next.

"Is there an infirmary here, too?" Del asks. "Maybe he's there?"

They slip back out into the increasingly chilly open air. The wind has a vicious bite to it— not so cold as where Del's journey began, but with a sharp dryness that leaves him trying to stop the chatter of his teeth.

A glance over at Kelsie gives him something else to worry about, on top of the increasingly ridiculous pile of concerns already present in his current predicament. The cold is as cruel against Kelsie's skin as it is against his own, and has left her face a chilly white and her cheeks flushed with two high, bright spots as vivid as cherries.

Boy or girl, hair spilled loose or hidden away, Kelsie is always very pretty. But with her colouring heightened to its current white-as-snow, red-as-blood confection, she is nothing short of heartbreaking.

Anyone who sees them won't be able to resist the opportunity to stop and talk to her. And if someone does that, it won't be long before they notice the long hair hidden away under the caps Kelsie and Del are wearing. They'll be found out as intruders and everything will plunge from 'bad' to 'horribly worse.'

Fear like a lump of lead in his stomach, Del follows Kelsie across a paved courtyard, then inside another building and up several long staircases. With every turn they make and corridor they navigate, Del imagines the discovery that surely awaits them any second now.

"This school is even less practical than mine," Kelsie notes as they finally approach the hospital wing. "Imagine how many sickly students have had to make this stupid trek while they've got horrid illnesses and are feeling wretched. Ugh."

At Kelsie's school, the infirmary rooms had been rather like doctor's offices. Here, they're closer to bedrooms. The first one that Del and Kelsie check is unoccupied and has the dank smell of somewhere shut up too long, of slightly sweaty skin.

In the second room, they find Nicholas.

He's sitting up in bed reading a paperback novel with a lurid sea monster attacking a pirate ship on the cover.

He looks incredibly puzzled to see them at first, two

strangers dressed in poorly-fitting uniforms and caps, but a split second later he recognises them and leaps out of bed to give Kelsie a hug.

Kelsie was surprisingly different from the last time Del remembered seeing her, but Nicholas is even more changed than that. He's taller, and his jaw has broadened ever so slightly from the gamine pixie chin he and his sister had shared in childhood.

The strongest memory that Del has of Nicholas, from when they were young, is of an autumn afternoon and feeling confused.

Del's never expected the world to make sense— who could, when working with magic every day— but it's been his experience that people each had their own internal consistency. He learned very early in his life how to predict what things would make the Ruby Warlock angry, so that he could avoid them.

Nicholas, however, remained a mystery, because of that one autumn afternoon when Del was fourteen.

The twins came home from school the same as usual: a little taller, older, and smarter, full of stories about friendships and lessons and dramas and adventures. Even after a few years to grow accustomed to the routine, Del still didn't quite know what to make of them— something he still found impossible even at seventeen. Kelsie and Nicholas were like something from another world, where growing up was entirely different.

Kelsie was friendly and funny, doing her best to stay as patient as she could while she reminded Del of how to play the old card games, and taught him new ones.

Nicholas started off by acting as he had in the past, ignoring Del for the most part and grudgingly tolerating him for the rest. The twins, despite being relative newcomers to the area, had made a solid mob of friends in the village, and Nicholas was usually to be found with them, being a nuisance in the square or hatching schemes out in the woods after being thrown out of the town proper by exasperated shopkeepers.

Autumn was a good time for ingredients— things were at their most potent for magic just when they stopped growing, before the cold. Del made trips back and forth between the village and the Ruby Warlock's house many times a day during the season, delivering the charms and unguents people had ordered.

One of these trips led him right past the group of boys lounging around the edge of the square's central fountain. They were all around the same age as him and Nicholas, but where Nicholas had joined their ranks with ease, Del wouldn't have the first idea of how to even talk to them, let alone make friends.

As he'd walked past, one of them had muttered something in a low voice and several of the others had snickered in reply, including one who sounded like Nicholas. Del didn't bother to react, or even to look over in their direction. He was used to it; the only thing that was different during the holidays was the number of voices in the laughter.

Another quiet comment and more laughing, but this time the Nicholas voice said, "come on, that's—" before trailing off. In the sharp reply that followed, Del heard the word 'freak', but anything after that was cut off from ever being said by a scuffle and a loud splash.

Nicholas had shoved one of the others backwards into the chill water of the fountain, and was standing with one hand clenched in a fist, as if he was daring the others to say a word. None of them did.

Back at the house, though, Nicholas was even more quiet and surly than usual, and the next day it was time for the twins to go back to school.

All that was years ago, but somehow Del's never forgotten it. No other memory from before that day or since gave that moment by the fountain an understandable context. Nicholas didn't care whether Del was alive or dead, so why defend him against something as inconsequential as the daily cruelties of the village boys?

Maybe Nicholas wanted to keep the sport of insulting Del all to himself, and someone else having a go made him furious. Was that something people did, something they felt? Del had never heard of anything like that, but that didn't mean it wasn't true. There were lots of things he didn't know, especially about people.

Nicholas doesn't look noticeably different now to what he was like the last time Del saw him. He has the same locks of wavy gold-brown hair falling forward into his eyes, the same long-fingered hands and knobby wrists. His shirt collar isn't flattened properly, which is a long-held bad habit, always making Nicholas look hurried and careless as a result. Del is faintly impressed that Nicholas manages to exhibit this same quirk even whilst clad in pajamas.

But the familiar things about Nicholas, the similarities in his appearance to earlier times, just make it even more obvious that something's wrong. Very wrong.

It's in the way his shoulders hunch, in how his eyes dart. Nicholas has the air of a prey animal about him, a squirrel or a hare. A creature always on the watch for the snapping jaw of razor teeth to close around it.

When Nicholas looks up at them from his book, Del catches sight of the graphite-grey tracery of veins in his throat, faint and fine and colourless as pencil-shading. Del's seen that before, on the wrists and arms of other children—apprentices and servants he's know, who hunched their shoulders and observed the world with sharp bright eyes.

To see that uncanny grey under Nicholas's skin makes something hot and fierce that Del doesn't have a name for flare and spit in his chest, a fire determined to get out.

"You came," Nicholas says, his voice muffled from being buried against his sister's shoulder. He sounds grateful and tired and young.

After a moment his shoulders stiffen and he steps back, holding Kelsie at arm's length. "You shouldn't have come. It's not... you shouldn't be here."

"Of *course* I came." She frowns, eyes narrowing as she stares at him. "Nicky, I—"

Nicholas is frowning too, his lips a tense line. "Kels," he says in a warning tone. Then his posture deflates; a clear surrender to the fact of her presence. "Thank you for coming to visit me."

"Nicky, what the bloody hell is going on? What's—"

"Why'd you bring him?" Nicholas asks, nodding his sharp chin in Del's direction. "He's too important and special to bother with the likes of us. Why would a clever wizard-in-training care about a couple of pathetic children? He—"

"Stop!" Kelsie snaps, cutting off her brother's mocking words. "He ran away to come help you! Stop being like this!"

"Is that true?" Nicholas asks Del.

"I ran away," Del confirms, because that much *is* the truth.

Mollified by the answer, or maybe just bored with the interrogation, Nicholas shrugs and looks away, scratching at the mark on his neck.

"You haven't answered my question," Kelsie reminds him, implacable steel in her voice.

There's a sound in the corridor, on the other side of the door at Del and Kelsie's backs. The three of them all start in surprise.

Nicholas's eyes widen and his gaze locks on Del's. There's stark terror in Nicholas's eyes as if he's afraid not about what's going to happen to him, what has been happening to him, but of the thought of having to tell Kelsie about it, of seeing her face as the knowledge sinks in.

The handle on the door turns and the hinges creak as they begin to swing open.

"Onto the roof. Quick," Nicholas orders them in a sharp voice.

There isn't time even for scrambling across the room and out over the sill. In the only moment afforded them,

Del waves his hand. The air gives a *crack*, smelling sharply of ozone as Del and Kelsie shrink down to sparrows. Their flight out the window is more wobbling than it is graceful, but the important thing is that it's faster than it would have been if they'd stayed as people.

They fly to sit atop the eave hanging over the window. Del makes them into themselves again, but keeps them the size of the birds they'd been. He's got yet another bloody nose for his trouble, and the cumulative effect of so many of them makes him lightheaded enough that he sits down and rests his head on his hands.

Their hiding spot abruptly goes dim, as someone inside the room draws the curtains closed.

The world is meant to look small from up high. People always describe it that way in stories. To Del the opposite has always felt true: when he's up high and can see so much of the world, he always feels tiny. A speck inside a huge and fast-moving universe. Tiny and very far away from everyone so far down below.

"You tell me *right now—*" Kelsie starts to say.

"Blood magic," Del interrupts her. "It's... it's blood magic."

Even the dim borrowed light from the window, Del can see how pale Kelsie's face goes at that. "Oh, well, that's not so terrible, is it?" she says with false brightness. "A little cut, or something like that? Nicky's had worse..."

"It's..." Del tries to think of a delicate way of phrasing it, of protecting her as much as possible. But he knows that if he tries, Kelsie will just stop and demand the full truth anyway.

"All magic is about energy," he tells her. "Most spell casters get it from small amounts of different things, mixed together. Mostly it's just elements in the air— scents, breath, sound, light. Sometimes it's ingredients, and when people use ingredients mixed up with mortar and pestle, the resulting mix will be a unique colour. No two magic users are the exact same shade; that's why no two of them have the same title."

"We covered that at school," Kelsie says. "The less powerful ones are things like turquoise and jade, then there's the middle level where they're garnet and ruby, and right up the tip are brownier ones like rust and jasper."

"Yes," Del agrees. He can still remember with stark clarity just how furious the Ruby Warlock had been when Del's colour turned out to be a ruddy ochre, at least two steps up in natural talent from the Warlock's own blue-tinged red. "Well... all those colours are words for substances that aren't alive, aren't they? Stones and minerals. But most of the really powerful colours, up the red-brown end, they're—"

"Amber or carmine or coral," Kelsie interrupts, bringing one hand up to cover her mouth in shock and disgust.

"Blood magic's not really about blood, blood's just the vessel for it, like water is in water magic, or air is in the magic you've seen me do. It plays a role, obviously, but the most important role it plays is as a conduit for energy. And in blood magic, that energy is—"

"Nicky," Kelsie finishes quietly. Del nods.

"I'll kill them." Kelsie's voice is soft and even and cold. "I'm going to kill them."

Since he's older than her, Del thinks he's probably supposed to give her a lecture at this point, to tell her all the reasons that she shouldn't want such a terrible thing as an opportunity to murder. But he doesn't know any way to say it that wouldn't ring hollow and false, so he just stays quiet.

"Why," Kelsie asks, so sad and quiet that Del wouldn't have heard her if he was any further away than right beside her. "Why would someone do that?"

"Blood magic can give the caster all of the stupid things you'd expect somebody like that to want," Del replies. "Power over other people, fame, wealth, youth, secrets. Think of anything greedy and selfish, and it's likely that you can take it from blood magic.

"It's not that there's anything inherently wicked about blood magic— there's nothing inherently anything about any kind of magic, just like there's nothing kind or cruel about the rain or the sunshine. It's all about what people do with them. But people who use blood magic nearly always use it for something terrible, because why else choose *that* instead of some other kind of spell?"

There's a greenish pallor to Kelsie's features now. "It sounds wicked to me. There's nothing neutral about stealing somebody else's *blood*."

"It doesn't have to be stolen. In fact, the magic is much more powerful if the blood is given freely than if it's taken. I'd say—" Del cuts himself off, biting his lip. Kelsie's eyes narrow.

"What were you going to say?"

"Nothing. It doesn't matter."

She presses her mouth into a thin pale frown. "Say it."

"Whoever it is doing it, they're probably making Nicholas cut his own skin. So that the magic's stronger. But magic isn't stupid. It would know that something like that can't be given freely, not in a circumstance like this."

The greenish tinge in Kelsie's face has given way to a marble-white cast on her features, pale and icy and implacable. Del looks away from her, desperate to give her some distraction from the thought of horrors.

"There's a bird's nest up over there," he says, gesturing to a chimney a few feet above them on the slope of the roof. "We're small enough to sleep in it, if you like. I don't think it's inhabited anymore. Or I can make it so we can jump down to the ground without getting hurt. That much I can do with this wand, anyway. It's a focus for my abilities, but it still needs to temper over time."

He's still talking when Kelsie shakes her head sharply. "I need to see. Make me a bird, so I can go closer to the window and look in at the edge of the curtain."

"But—" Del starts to object, before her expression makes him shut his mouth. This is not a discussion, or even a negotiation, as far as Kelsie's concerned.

"Make me a bird," she repeats, through gritted teeth.

"I'm not your servant anymore!" Del snaps in reply. Kelsie flinches like he's slapped her.

Before their argument can escalate, there's a high, frightened cry from inside— Nicholas's voice, but not as Del has ever heard it before.

Kelsie, looking terribly panicked and afraid, grabs one of Del's hands in both of her own. Her grip is bone-hard, hard enough that he wonders for a moment if it'll bruise.

"Please," she whispers.

So he makes her a bird, a sparrow the same deep honey-gold shade of brown as her hair, and Kelsie flits down to perch on the sill of her brother's window.

After all the casting Del's been doing lately, this isn't enough to make his nose bleed, but he feels sick and exhausted enough from the effort that he sits down on the roof again and decides to just wait for her right there.

It's the very darkest part of the night, now, but from this close to so many lights it's hard to see much in the way of stars above. Del hunts to catch a glimpse between the clouds anyway, to find the gleams bright enough that an entire school of lamps and candles can't dim their twinkle.

He wonders why Kelsie wrote to him. What reason she had for including him in their plans of escape.

It's idiotic, wondering about something like that. Even as he indulges in it, Del knows that it's idiotic. Kelsie asked for his help because of his magic, of course. There's no other possible reason. It's just her good luck that he was planning an escape of his own that coincided with her call for aid.

He wonders, just for a moment, if he would have come anyway if he hadn't had an urgency to propel him. If it had meant leaving behind his little life with its cellar and its chores and cold mornings.

But before he can decide one way or another, Del shakes himself out of his thoughts. There's no point in wondering about what might have happened if he'd read Kelsie's letter before overhearing the Ruby Warlock's conversation. Things are as they are, and wondering doesn't change anything.

After that, he just stares up at the stars and waits for Kelsie and tries not to think about anything at all.

When the Kelsie-sparrow comes up to rejoin him, Del doesn't turn her back right away. Instead, he tosses her pieces of bread from his pouch, small as crumbs in his current state, and lets her have a moment to just be a bird.

Once she's human again, she sits beside him and uses her fingers to comb out the tangles in her hair, then smooths creases out of her trousers with almost-steady palms. She doesn't say anything, worrying her lower lip between her teeth as she very carefully adjusts every fold and hem and pocket of her clothes.

"You can cry if you want. I've cast a silencing cone around us. Nobody will hear," Del assures her.

Kelsie's head whips up again, the same struck look on her face as when Del had snapped that he wasn't her servant anymore. Her eyes narrow.

"You don't know us at all, do you?" she asks in an even voice, dangerously quiet.

"No," Del answers. "Not really. Only card games and holidays."

"And even those didn't mean the same things to you that they did to us," Kelsie says softly, sounding small and hollow and alone.

He feels bad for causing that, especially considering the rest of the situation they've managed to find themselves in. The last thing Kelsie needs is to feel that she and her brother are trusting themselves to a magic-user who doesn't even like them.

Del likes them just fine. He just doesn't know them very well.

"What do you want to do next?" he asks her. Del's never had the knack of knowing the right thing to say to comfort someone or make them feel better. He hopes planning their escape will distract Kelsie from her sadness.

"Kill him. I told you that," she tells him. "Did you think that I was joking?"

Del shakes his head. "No. I knew you weren't. But murdering a person, especially someone larger and stronger than you are, isn't some small thing. We'll still need to think of a plan, whether it's for escape or for, um, that."

Kelsie smiles. There is nothing warm or sweet about the expression.

"I already have one," she says. "And don't worry. I won't be murdering anyone."

She's polite enough to give him a new handkerchief for his nose, before they break into the teacher's room.

The lock on the door is simple enough that Kelsie cracks it with a hairpin and a few minutes' fiddling. They open the door as quietly as they can and creep inside.

They aren't quiet enough. The man sits up in bed as they step inside, the blurriness of sleep dissipating from his eyes as he stares at the intruders. Del's heart thuds with fear, arms and legs going cold in a rush.

"Do it," Kelsie says, her voice as chill as Del's blood feels. Confusion gives way to anger in the teacher's face as Del raises his hand, new wand gripped tight in the curl of his fist.

What they're doing is monstrous, really. But Del can't find it in himself to feel guilty. And if his own agreement to the plan is a passive compliance, then Kelsie's masterminding of it is an active defiance of caring about things like being monstrous or taking away somebody's humanity and agency.

The energy of revenge makes for incredibly powerful, chaotic magic. The little wooden stick in Del's hand feels like it's writhing against his skin, lashing with the strength of the energy coursing through it.

In what feels like no time at all, a swirling split-second

of wildness that Del and Kelsie can barely stand against, let alone control, the spell is done. On the bed, where a moment before the man had been, is a spider. .

It's the size of a loaf of bread, thick-bodied and covered in wiry brown hair. Del's skin crawls at the sight of it, at the glassy black sheen of its myriad eyes blinking awake and its long hairy legs jerking and writhing in their first awkward movements.

Kelsie grabs one of the legs, the spindly joint thicker than her thumb. She's back to her usual girl-body now, and her movements are graceless and brutal as she shoves the creature into the pillowcase in her other hand. Del tries to stop the blood coming out of his nose from getting all over the floor or the bedding— the last thing they need is to make the place look like a crime scene.

She ties a knot at the end of the pillowcase, trapping the creature inside, and drops the twitching little cotton sack to the floor. Without a word, she begins to kick and stamp. Her boots make soft thuds which are drowned out almost completely by the rattling, hissing, screeching sounds the spider makes as she kills it. Her eyes are shiny-bright with wetness, but she doesn't cry, doesn't make a sound. Her face is very pale, except for two spots of high colour on her cheeks, like those on a fever victim.

By the time the pillowcase has stopped moving, and dark spots have begun to seep through the lumpy shape of the cotton, Del realises that he and Kelsie have both been holding their breath. Kelsie lets out a long sigh, her shoulders slumping as tension gives way to weary defeat in her posture. Del breathes out along with her, and only then notices Nicholas leaning against the door frame.

There's a new bruise high on one of his cheeks, the red and purple bloom of it blotting out the sight of the delicate freckles that Del knows are usually scattered across that thin skin. He's clearly more prone to crying than his sister— his eyes are red and raw with it, and the patrician paleness of his nose is spoiled a little by blotchy redness from blowing.

He's watching the pair of them, his damp-lashed eyes unreadable as they flit between Del's face, and Kelsie's, and the pillowcase on the floor. Awkwardly, Del picks it up by the knot before the blood can seep through and stain the carpet underneath.

"I suppose I should gather some clothes," Nicholas remarks, voice as blank as his expression. "I'll meet you downstairs in a few minutes. That'll give you time to get rid of the mess you've made."

Del bristles, frowning in annoyance. It isn't that he thinks Nicholas should *thank* them for committing murder to avenge mistreatment against him, but... well, all right. Maybe Del did expect a thank-you, as stupid as that sounds. Something a little bit more grateful than a sardonic quip about making a mess, at least.

Kelsie sees his expression and smacks him lightly on the back of the hand holding the pillowcase. "Don't you start being stupid too. Come on, we've got to hurry and get rid of this."

Getting back downstairs and out of the school grounds is worse than breaking in had been. The pillowcase grows heavier in Del's hands the longer he has to carry it, which is exhausting. But the more exhausted he gets, the more the enchantment wavers and fades, and that makes the spider-body inside weigh more and more as it tries to revert to its natural state. Dead things don't stay transformed without constant attention.

Kelsie manages to pry up a paving stone, right where two pathways across the courtyard cross.

"Site of protection," she explains to Del, panting from the exertion. "The dead don't come back when they're buried at crossroads."

"I don't think we have to worry about that," Del says.

Kelsie shrugs one shoulder.

"Probably not. But it doesn't hurt to be sure," she says as she and takes the pillowcase from him. The unexpected weight of it makes her 'oof' in surprise, and she hauls it into the space where the stone had been. With an unceremonious shove, she replaces the paving, crushing the spider underneath.

Del is bone weary. The excitements of the last day coupled with the fact that he's done far more complex magic— and bled many times as a result— than ever before, have left him feeling utterly drained.

He almost wishes that it was him under the paving slab, that he had nothing left to worry about and nowhere left to go.

No point in thoughts like that, though. They still have a long way left to go.

Dawn is lending slow grey light to the world around them by the time the three of them are ready to go, their bags full up with stolen food from the kitchen, even though none of them have any kind of appetite. Del knows that they'll need the energy from food to keep up a good walking pace, but despite the sense and practicality of insisting that they all eat he can't bring himself to say anything. Being hungry for one day is unlikely to be the thing that thwarts their escape. And no matter how weary Del feels, he... he can't eat. Not right now. Not yet.

Nicholas manages four hours of walking before he faints. The complete lack of melodrama exhibited— he just drops into a crumple on the muddy ground between one step and the next— is the thing that frightens Del and Kelsie the most.

They get him sitting up and Kelsie gives him sips from her water bottle. The colourless pallor in Nicholas's cheeks is too close to the drained grey he'd had at the school. It makes Del feel helpless and angry.

Children are playing a noisy game, somewhere close enough that their shouts are in earshot.

"I'll be back soon," Del promises the twins, and heads towards the noise.

It's a cottage, with a vegetable garden in long rows beside it and a lady with white hair shelling peas on the front stoop. Children are chasing one another across the open field next to the house, playing a game with no obvious objective or rules. A bemused cow stands in the middle of the open grass and ignores the shrieks around her.

"Good morning, ma'am," Del says to the lady. "I'm..."

He's not very good at asking for help. Doing that has been something Del has staunchly avoided in his life, and so it doesn't come easily to him even when he needs to.

"My friend needs to rest for a while," he says finally. Truth will have to stand in for manners. "If he can lie down inside your house, my other friend and I will help you with chores until he's recovered."

"It's not contagious, is it? Octavia— she's my youngest— isn't a hearty lass. I won't have her exposed to fevers or chills."

Del shakes his head. "No, nothing like that. It's not catching. He's just weak."

"Mm, all right then," she agrees with a nod. "Bring him over."

"He's not... always polite," Del warns, as diplomatic as possible.

"I can survive without polite," says the lady. "Polite has nothing to do with whether a person's good or bad. Is he good?"

Del remembers the splash of the fountain in the village square, in an autumn long ago.

"I think so," he answers.

Del goes back to Nicholas and Kelsie, and the three of them make their way to the cottage at a slow, unsteady pace. Nicholas refuses to rest against either of them, but with just his own feet to carry him he's halting and unsteady.

When they get there the lady— who introduces herself as Philomena, and doesn't ask them what their own names are— bundles Nicholas inside and sits him in a large rocking chair with blankets and a cup of tea.

"I've got two jobs that need doing: peeling potatoes or chopping firew—"

"I'll do firewood," Kelsie states before Philomena's even finished talking. Which leaves Del to pick up a knife and a potato, sitting down on the stoop beside Philomena as the children keep on playing their game.

A while later, one of the children darts over to where Philomena and Del are sitting, appearing out of nowhere from around the side of the building. The little girl crouches, giggling, behind the scraps barrel.

"You Princess Aria, then?" Philomena asks. The girl nods, her delighted grin showing off a missing front tooth.

"A hide-and-seek game?" Del asks. Philomena's words have stirred a dark, panicked feeling in him, making his heart beat double-fast and his hands shake. He's never liked games where the players wear different names to fit their roles. Somehow that feels very different than disguises, in a way he wouldn't know how to articulate if asked. A name is who you *are*. Disguises are just who other people *think* you are.

That's why he doesn't like being called Rowan. That doesn't happen very often, but when it does it always strikes him as a fundamental wrongness. He's not Rowan. He's Del.

"Aye. One girl hides— like Octavia Elizabeth here— and all the boys have to race around and look for her. If two of them run into each other in the meantime, they have to have a scuffle to see who's dead and who gets to keep on looking. The lad who finds Princess Aria is the Prince, and wins."

"Sometimes they try to kiss me," Octavia says, clearly disgusted. "And I never get to be anyone but the Princess, because I'm a girl. If I want to play, it's this or nothing." She sighs, her happy smile momentarily becoming a mournful frown.

"Well, you just stay hiding there and those boys will have all killed each other long before you're found," Philomena assures her.

"Octavia Elizabeth is a big name for a little girl," Del remarks. "Very grand."

Octavia wrinkles her nose. “Not really. ‘Dandelion’ is a big word but that don’t make it grand; they’re too common for that. I’m only Octavia Elizabeth so as to tell me apart from Octavia Rose who lives near the mill, and Octavia Alexandra and Octavia Dora over the river. We’re only as fancy as dandelions, really. Common as weeds.”

When Nicholas is strong enough to set off walking again, Del offers Philomena some of the food they stole from the school as a thank you.

"No need to give up what you can't spare, not just for use of shade and a comfortable chair," she tells him. "Learn to take things when they're offered, without worrying about how to even out the score. Life tends to find a way to pay you back what you've earned, and charge for what you've bought from it."

They stay in the forest and off the paths until well after nightfall, keeping their pace a fraction slower for Nicholas's sake. When the passing traffic of people on horseback and on foot, and carriages and carts, has slowed to nothing, they emerge out onto the road. After hours of picking their way through knotted roots and branches, stumbling into creeks and getting feet caught in burrow entrances, the level pebbled pathway is a luxury even in the almost total dark.

"Can't you make the clouds part, so we've got starlight at least?" Nicholas complains, scuffing his shoe against the grass on the edge of the path to clean off yet another horse dropping that he's stepped in.

"I'm as tired as you are," Del warns. "That makes magic unstable. We might end up rained on if I try to push the wind. I'm not going to risk that just so you don't step in things."

"*Now* you're worried about being responsible and careful?" Nicholas retorts, sullen and sarcastic. "I bet if Kelsie asked, you would."

"*Fine,*" Del says through gritted teeth. "*Here.*"

He holds his little stick-wand above his head and chants a short rhyme.

There's an ominous rumble of thunder and a few small zaps of lightning, like the sky is reminding them of the near-limitless power they're trying to influence. But the downpour Del feared doesn't follow the warning, and after a few moments the heavy grey-black clouds have parted enough that they can see the stars and moon.

The thin silvery light washes Del and Kelsie and Nicholas, and the road and the forest around them, and makes them at least a little visible to one another.

"Thank you," Kelsie says. Nicholas just makes a small grunting sound and picks up his walking pace.

Del shrugs at Kelsie, not sure how he's expected to respond to her thanks.

The night goes quickly after that, the road remaining easily navigable over miles of hills and fields and orchards and woods. When their appetites return they argue about whether to climb a fence to steal some fruit or vegetables, or even a few eggs from a chicken coop, but in the end they decide not to. They're still too close to Nicholas's school, and they don't want anyone to guess which direction they're heading.

Hungry and tired, they leave the road again as the sun rises, and make their way into the forest.

"What about that tree?" Nicholas suggests, pointing to a hollow trunk large enough to fit the three of them.

They manage to settle in comfortably enough with Kelsie taking the middle so that Nicholas and Del will stop complaining about being jabbed with each other's skinny elbows.

It's not actually so bad, being squashed up together like that, because it keeps them warm and makes everything that's happened feel a little less huge and frightening. It doesn't take long before Del's eyes slide closed and he falls into a deep sleep.

He wakes in the mid-afternoon, and gently shakes

Kelsie awake. If he could reach, he'd shake Nicholas awake too— probably a little less gently— but there isn't a lot of room to move inside the hollow until Kelsie wriggles out into the open air, and by then Nicholas has woken of his own accord.

They walk a few hours more, until twilight. By now even Kelsie is snappish with hunger, and they all feel grimy and stiff and sore from their sleeping arrangements.

In the next big valley there's a small village. It's not impressive, not compared to the larger and more prosperous village that the Ruby Warlock lived near, but to three tired teenagers the golden rectangles of light in the few windows are so welcoming that Kelsie lets out of a little gasp of exhausted delight at the sight of them.

The tavern is warm in the chill evening, and smells comfortingly of wood smoke inside. It makes Del think of his snug little cellar room, and he lets himself feel one small, sweet pang of homesickness before pushing the thought aside and paying for three plates of cheese and bread, and three mugs of wine.

For a while they don't make conversation, concentrating instead on eating as much as they can as fast as they can.

"Ordinary food tastes different than magical food," Kelsie eventually says, breaking the silence. She sounds surprised at the discovery.

"Does it?" Nicholas asks.

Del blinks at the two of them, confused for a moment before he realises that Kelsie never had reason to eat magical food before the bread he'd fed her as a sparrow, and Nicholas has never eaten it at all.

Del thinks of all the nights when he'd had to stir up a final reserve of energy out of his aching young body to conjure up a cup of soup or a ham sandwich before crawling into bed, having been given nothing by the Ruby Warlock during the day.

He tries to feel glad on the twins' behalf, that they've never been in that position. It's hard to work up a particularly enthusiastic charitable impulse in that regard.

"Yes," Kelsie answers her brother, interrupting Del's train of thought before he feels too bitter or jealous. The past is the past. It doesn't matter now— they're all stuck in the same predicament. "Not better or worse, or anything like that. Just different."

"Magical food isn't as filling, even if it feels like it is," Del tells her. "If you only ever ate conjurations, you'd die of starvation soon enough."

"Well, we've got enough money to buy proper food for a while yet, so we'll be all right," she says. She's turning her hand back and forth, looking at the palm with a perplexed expression. "My scar's gone."

"The one from when you got your finger caught in the spinning wheel?" Nicholas asks.

Kelsie nods.

"Yes. I had a great horrid scar right across the pad of my finger, from where it got pinched. But it's gone now."

"You switched from girl to boy and back again. That always heals anything hurt," Del explains around a mouthful of cheese. After swallowing, he drinks a mouthful of wine, and then looks up at the twins. They're both staring at him, something like pity on their faces.

He bristles at the look, trying not to scowl too obviously and only partly succeeding. "What?"

"You don't have any scars?" Kelsie asks.

"No." Del shakes his head. "Oh, well. I have this." He touches the grey lock of hair above his temple. "That stays, no matter what I turn into. I don't know why."

The room they rent is standard fare for cheap lodgings: a fireplace, a washstand and chamber pot, a window rheumy with frost, and a wide bed.

"Sleeps five grown men in a row, that one does," the innkeeper tells them. That might be stretching the truth somewhat, in Del's opinion, but it's certainly enough space for three small teenagers.

Yet when they're done unlacing their boots and washing

their faces, Del feels a strange apprehension at the thought of being so vulnerable in front of the twins. It's not that he doesn't trust them, it's just that a proper bed— however lumpy and scratchy and questionably clean— will mean he might finally get a proper rest, might fall asleep in a way not possible in hollow trees.

Del has never let anybody see him like that, so unguarded and defenceless. He isn't ready for Nicholas and Kelsie to see it now, not when he needs for them to think of him as powerful and useful and fundamental to their escape.

He can't risk losing them, which means he can't let himself go and collapse into deep slumber.

Del sits down on the floor, his back resting against the door. "Better for my back," he explains to the quizzical Kelsie.

She looks skeptical. "There's lots of room..."

"No, really, I'm fine.

"Let him be uncomfortable if he wants," Nicholas says in a breezy voice, climbing into bed on the far side from the door. "It's no skin off our noses if he enjoys being stupid."

Kelsie gives her brother an irritated glance, but doesn't attempt to persuade Del again. She turns down the lamp to nothing but the faintest amber glow and climbs into the other side of the bed.

The wind outside makes the panes of glass in the window rattle. Del draws his knees up to his chest and waits for morning.

They eat bread and cheese and dried apple for breakfast, and buy more to carry with them. The air is cold and clear, the morning cloudless and bright.

Despite his near-sleepless night, Del discovers he's in quite a good mood. He's smiling as they set off.

A few hours later, halfway up a steep hill— "More like a mountain," grumbles Nicholas— they begin to come across rubble.

Del ignores his complaining. Nicholas should have found some more comfortable shoes to run away in. Del's not going to waste valuable energy performing a spell to fix the problem.

The rubble isn't anything much at first, just a brick here and there, a couple of thick wooden beams that are blackened from a long-ago fire. As they get higher up, the debris becomes more frequent. A cracked ceramic pot, now irretrievably entangled with the vines and roots of the forest floor. The iron lacework gate from a long-vanished fence, half eaten by rust.

"It's a church yard," Kelsie says as they move past the old gate. "Look, see? The headstones."

The ground is flatter here, but not by much. It seems a curious place for a graveyard and a church.

The two boys trail behind as Kelsie catches sight of the remains of the building itself. The walls are little more than low uneven lines of grey stone bricks, a rectangle of space as wild and overrun with plants as the world around it.

"Oh, how pretty," Kelsie murmurs, moving in close to look at what must have once been the crown jewel of the little church, a leadlight stained-glass window . The glass is shattered down to shards, jewel-like chips as big as a knucklebone.

"Seems like you've still got a little of the bird about you," Del teases. "Drawn to shiny things."

Nicholas sits down on the remains of the wall, using the crumbled stonework as a chair as he eases one shoe off and rubs at his blisters. Del crosses to the other side of the area that used to be indoors, looking around to see if anything of value has survived. They might be able to sell it. Money's going to start being a concern eventually, so it's better if Del starts thinking about it now.

"Aaah!"

The panicked shout of surprise comes from Nicholas, who's back on his feet and standing as if ready for a fight by the time Del turns to face them.

Kelsie darts to her brother's side, touching him on the arm.

They're always physically in sync with one another, on an instinctive level. Del hopes that closeness won't be a liability if they're ever seriously endangered.

"A wolf. Or a dog. I don't— something big. Over there," Nicholas says, pointing a shaking hand towards the forest around them.

"A kyrke grim," Del tells him, coming to stand near the pair. The creature has vanished from sight. "Looks like you won't be able to take any of the glass with you, Kelsie."

"A what?" she asks. "And why not?"

"You might have heard them called a shuck, or a gwyllgi, instead. And you can't take the glass because it's his. The whole church is his. He guards it."

"Shucks are evil, though," Nicholas says scornfully, never taking his eyes off the now-empty patch of space between two trees. "Big black dogs with red eyes that lure travellers off the road? What's one of those want with an old fallen-down church?"

"It's dangerous?" Kelsie asks, fear and determination equally present in her voice, as if she intends to square off against it herself if it proves to be a threat.

"Not to everyone," Del tells her. "Not always.

"When this church was built," he goes on, "the townspeople would have believed that the soul of the first person buried in the graveyard would be reborn after death as a guardian of the cemetery and the church and the surrounding land.

"So, to save anybody from being stuck with that job, when the church was being built they would have killed a lamb and buried it under the altar. Its soul became the kyrke grim. So even if religion isn't really here anymore, there's still the protection of the grim."

Kelsie steps into the church, walking across the empty spaces where there's nothing left but rubble and leaves, running her fingertips along the back of the old, smoothed wood of the pews. "It feels... fierce, but friendly," she says after a few moments. "Protective. A lot like ordinary dogs, but *bigger* somehow."

"I can't feel it at all," Nicholas says.

Kelsie gives him a crooked grin. "Of course you can't. You can't even dowse," she teases.

That makes him roll his eyes. "Magic's all pathetic garbage anyway. Killing lambs to keep ruined churches safe, swapping eyes like they're marbles or knucklebones in a schoolyard game. It's all stupid."

"How admirable of you not to be bitter or jealous," Del remarks, keeping his voice as deadpan as he can. The glare he earns from Nicholas for his words is as nasty and sharp as daggers.

They spend the rest of the daylight on exploring the ruins. Kelsie takes up residence in the half-rotted little booth that was once a confessional, her nimble fingers playing with the soft wood of the lattice as she mutters to herself quietly.

Del and Nicholas both make a point of moving to the other end of the church, where the cracked marble altar has been knitted over with a thick tangle of vines and roots. From here, they can't hear Kelsie's words, only the cadence of her voice as she whispers and murmurs whatever pleas for forgiveness she feels she owes the world.

As they unpack their sparse bedding and blankets for the night, Nicholas beckons his sister over to the same stained glass rubble which first caught her eye. Del wanders over as well, and finds the twins staring down at a tiny brown spider perched on a little shard of a green panel from the window.

"It's almost like a sign, isn't it?" Nicholas remarks. "That's spider's just the same as... just the same as another one."

"Mm," Kelsie says, her mouth thinning into a frown for a moment at the dark memory. "I'd love... do you think this means it would be all right?" She addresses the question to Del. "Do you think the spider means that it's all right for me to take some, just a tiny bit?"

He knows she wants reassurance, but the only honest answer Del can offer is a shrug. That earns him a withering look from Nicholas, but Kelsie seems to have made up her mind even without Del's encouragement. She waits until the spider has moved away, then picks up the green glass shard between her thumb and forefinger, tilting it so some of the edges catch the light and sparkle.

Kelsie pulls a small suede pouch out of her satchel, the sort often used for storing money. It's dyed a brilliant crimson colour and decorated with an embroidered design of leaves and twisting vines in vivid oranges and golds. She pulls the drawstring open and slips the little treasure inside.

"I can make the inside of that bigger for you, if you want," Del offers.

"No," Kelsie answers, slipping the pouch back into her satchel. "It's fine like this."

Too exhausted to explore anymore but also too keyed-up to sleep, Del sits down by the small fire they've built and fetches his dice out of the recesses of his own, more internally expansive, pouch. The dice are made of blue granite, tiny chips of gleaming crystal and trace metals visible in each of the smooth-polished sides.

One of the dice is made of a paler stone than the other, so Del begins to roll them both together, counting which has the higher number on each turn.

"You shouldn't play with those in church," chides Nicholas. His thin, fox-like face is stained red-gold by the firelight as he frowns at Del.

"The Coral Sorcerer. A wizard who... who wanted to buy me from your step-father," Del says, forcing himself to speak the truth of the situation aloud as he gazes down at the little toys. "He loves dice. All kinds of gambling. He's the one who taught me all the dice games I know. He can never resist a chance to play them, even if it's only against an apprentice he has to teach the rules to. He told me that he's never lost a game of any kind. Not a single one."

"I could beat him," Kelsie's sleepy voice declares from beyond the fire's periphery.

Nicholas snorts in disbelief. "You can believe that if you want. You're hardly invincible. I've won enough times against you to know that."

"Maybe I was just letting you win," says Kelsie.

They set out early the next morning and reach the shoreline before noon. Without the mountain to act as a levee against the ocean winds, they face much colder air on the trek down from the peak than they did on the way up from the village, but nobody complains very much.

Of course, in Nicholas's case, that's a relative concept and actually entails a fair amount of complaining.

The sea breeze is refreshing against Del's face, as if he's finally able to breathe in after days and days of hardly daring to inhale for fear of upsetting the delicate balances of their escape. "What now?" Nicholas asks, when they're finally standing on the weathered wood of the docks, all the bustle of the little port going on around them. The air is sea and salt and fish and creaking ships and crying seagulls.

"Now we find a boat," Kelsie says firmly. "And we go somewhere else."

"I really appreciate the specificity you always bring to your plans," Del deadpans. "Really."

Nicholas tries to bite down on a smile as Kelsie huffs, annoyed. "All right then," she challenges. "*You* work out our next step."

"I'll do it," says Nicholas, taking his hands out of his pockets and glancing at the other people around them. The man he chooses to approach has a bristly beard of white and grey, a blue knit wool cap on his head against the chill, and a faded tracery of blue tattoos up both his forearms and under his sleeves, mermaids and swallows and sunsets and ships.

"Do you know if anyone's got boats for sale?" Nicholas asks. His tone's not rude, but it isn't exactly friendly either.

The man looks up from the coil of rope he's winding and gives Nicholas an amused, close-lipped smile, before nodding at Del and Kelsie standing behind.

"I hope you didn't get picked to be the talky one because you're the most polite," the sailor says, laughing at his own joke.

Nicholas scowls. "Don't make fun of me."

"Don't be so funny, then. And aye, there's a dory I can spare. Might suit you three well enough, if it's just doing jaunts around the islands that you're plannin.' It ain't new, so there's a few stains from this and that, but nothing corrosive. It's seaworthy enough. And gunpowder, too, spilled on its floor, from a salvage trip I did out to one of the big wrecks out past the Coal Isle. Careful of that."

Nicholas crosses his arms, an unimpressed expression on his face. "Sounds awful. Don't you have anything without so much wrong with it?"

That just makes the fisherman laugh heartily again. He has shiny white teeth and a booming belly laugh. "What a sour lad you are! Come on, come and take a look at it. Might be that the world's not out to cheat you and do you wrong quite so constantly as you expect of it."

The boat is a deep, vivid blue, and, with the wavering sunlight playing against the hull in bright crisscrosses, it looks as if the little craft is a part of the water itself, a vessel grown up out of the tides by a magic stranger than any Del knows.

"We'll take it," Nicholas tells the fisherman as soon as they lay eyes on it, earning himself another hearty laugh.

The little boat wobbles as they climb in. Kelsie doesn't seem worried by this fact and so Del tries not to panic either, but this is the first time he can remember ever being in a boat and the motion makes him feel unstable and strange.

Nicholas laughs at Del's caution. "That's just how dories are. It's the down-side of them being shaped this way, with the high sides and flat floor and sharp bows."

"Nicky's done sailing at school," Kelsie explains. "You

were rather good at it, weren't you?"

Nicholas shrugs in reply, pulling hard on a rope. His action makes the mast unfold to its full height. "It's nice for me to be the one who knows how to do something for a change."

"Oh, we could probably make it work with magic, if we had to," Kelsie retorts.

"Actually, no, we couldn't," Del corrects her. "The ocean doesn't react well to magic. Years ago, before your mother married the Ruby Warlock, there was a bad drought. A group of spellcasters all gathered together to go out in a boat and cast spells at sea because they knew it would create a violent storm which they could then blow in the right direction and make it rain where the drought was.

"That's where the wrecks near the Coal Isle come from. The wizards forgot to warn everyone about what they were planning. A lot of people died. Some say it was more people than were saved by the rain, but there's no way to know that for sure."

"See?" Nicholas says to Kelsie in a pointed tone. "I told you. Magic's awful."

"Not really. Just some of the people who use it are," Del answers, but Nicholas ignores him.

They make good time getting out of the harbour— Nicholas is very good at piloting the little boat— and soon they're well on the way to the first of the little islands which scatter across the coast for a hundred miles in either direction.

"Sometimes when I was young, I'd pretend that I was born on a boat," Del admits to Kelsie, as they try to collect and dispose of some of the spilled gunpowder underfoot. "A son of a gun, like in pirate stories. Born with my mother's back braced against a cannon on a deck somewhere."

"Little boys who grow up wizards dream of being pirates," Kelsie says with a smile. "Nobody's ever happy with the hand they're dealt."

Del smiles back. "No, I suppose not."

"We're not really so different," Nicholas cuts in, speaking to his sister as he steers their craft. "Remember the games we used to play, imagining who our father might have been? Even though we knew from mother just about everything there was to know. Think of how much more imagining we would have done if we'd had no idea about him."

Kelsie looks surprised. "You don't know anything about your mother?" she asks Del. He shrugs.

"No. Nothing. And the stories I was told all contradicted one another, so I've no idea if any of them are true."

"Have you ever had anybody who was *like* one for you? We had an uncle; he was all right. I know mother's not much of a step-mother to you, but..."

"I don't know," Del says, wishing he was the sort of person who could make up a lie, because now Kelsie's looking sad again and he doesn't like it when she looks like that. "The Ruby Warlock's been married twice, in my memory, but my memory's terrible. You know that. Who knows what I've forgotten?"

"Or pretended to have forgotten, like the card games," Nicholas mutters, and Kelsie's too busy glaring at her brother for the jab to keep looking sadly at Del.

"Not that again," Kelsie sighs. "Can't we have one nice day in the sunshine without the two of you fighting like cats?"

Neither Del nor Nicholas dignifies her question with a response. She goes back to tipping handfuls of gunpowder overboard for a little while.

"This gunpowder's magical. Just a little bit. A slight charge," Del notes. "Sometimes that happens. Things just naturally build up a bit, for no reason anybody knows."

Kelsie looks down at the grit clinging to her palm, which is soon whisked away by the brisk wind.

"What parlour games do magicians play?" she asks Del. "Do they have special ones, ones that need spells?"

"Not exactly," Del tells her. "But there are games that

only magic users can play, yes. The one children learn first, after dowsing of course." He aims a sly smirk at Nicholas, who humphs and pretends to be absorbed in his work at the sail "It's the scales game. Here, I'll show you."

"Wait! Aren't we supposed to avoid magic when we're on the ocean?" Kelsie stops him.

Del shakes his head. "No, it should be all right, so long as nothing I conjure touches the water. The sea doesn't care about magic being done *near* it, only magic being done *to* it."

He waves a hand to conjure a set of scales into being, the sort used by apothecaries and bank managers to weigh medicines or gold, and leaves it hanging in mid-air so that the rocking of the boat won't cause unsteadiness.

"It's a little bit like a guessing game, but the better you are at sensing magic, the less guessing is involved," explains Del. "So children play it to get better and better at distinguishing the potency of ingredients."

He pulls the little container of powdered snakeskin out of his pouch. "See, I put this on one side..." He taps a small mound of the reagent onto one of the scale's two dishes. "And now you have to match it to as close to a balance as you can. If you can manage, then the point goes to you. If you don't, the point goes to me."

Kelsie tilts her head to one side, staring hard at the tiny pile of snakeskin powder. Then she drops down into a crouch, scoops up a half-handful of the gritty gunpowder scattered there, and lets it fall on the second dish of the scales. The pile is much, much larger than that of snakeskin, but the scales only wobble back and forth before coming to rest at a level that's very close to even.

"Hm. Not bad, for my first try," Kelsie says critically. "I wasn't sure if the physical weight played into it at all. Next time, I'll compensate for that."

"So the gunpowder has a little bit of magic, but not as much as that other stuff?" Nicholas asks, clearly fascinated, his new makeshift fishing line bobbing forlornly on the surface of the water and completely ignored as he watches Kelsie and Del's game.

"Yes," Del says with a nod. "That's right. Kelsie had a little advantage, because I was talking earlier about how this gunpowder had a mild charge to it, but it's still a solid first go."

Nicholas continues to stare at the suspended scales for a few more seconds, but when Del waves a hand and vanishes the whole setup from existence, Nicholas's face falls into a frown again and he turns away.

"It's all just party tricks. Can't see that there's anything I'm missing out on."

Kelsie sighs. "Don't be like that." It looks just the same as it always has when she rolls her eyes, even though her eyes are really Del's eyes now, since they haven't bothered swapping back.

"I'll trade a hand with you," Del offers, because he knows that if he doesn't say something then Nicholas is going to sulk for who knows how long, and the boat isn't nearly big enough to accommodate a bad mood. "So you can try it. For a little while."

Nicholas looks at Del suspiciously. "Why would you do that?"

"Because in a few minutes I'm going to throw you both overboard and leave you to drown!" Kelsie says, sounding half-serious about the threat.

"It'll be the right hand. I'm left-handed, and I don't want to give up that one, even it's just for a few minutes," Del says. "So if you're right-handed, you won't be able to write letters properly or anything, since I'll be switching your dominant hand for a non-dominant one."

"That's all right. I'm left-handed too," Nicholas answers, climbing to his feet. The dory rocks back and forth a little as if it's scolding them for moving around so much instead of staying put like proper passengers. "So is it really a swap? Or is it... I don't know. I don't even know what to ask you about it!" he laughs, amused at his own ignorance.

Del can't remember the last time he heard Nicholas truly laugh. It might have been a year ago or even longer. The sound has grown deeper since then. There's a barb to it, like even ordinary simply amusement always has a catch for Nicholas now. It should make the laughter less appealing, Del thinks, and yet somehow it does the opposite— the bitter undertone makes the sweetness of the rest of it even lighter.

"It's easier if one of us is holding something," says Del.

Nicholas pulls a compass from his pocket, a tiny thing decorated with a scrimshaw cameo on its lid.

"Yes, that's good. Hold it tight in your fist and put your hand out... good."

Del curls his own hand into an empty mirror of Nicholas's and concentrates hard on the idea of holding the compass, of his hand already holding it, of his hand being over *there* when it should be over *here*...

He opens his eyes.

Nicholas curls and uncurls the fingers of his new right hand. "How strange," he murmurs, then looks up at Del. "I can feel it, but I can also faintly feel you there." He gestures to where Del holds the compass with Nicholas's own slim borrowed fingers. "Like an echo."

Del nods. "You'll get used to it soon. Think of it as a phantom limb— like sailors who've lost a leg but still swear they feel aching in that foot, even though there's really only a peg there."

"If we'd stowed away on a big ship," Kelsie muses. "One with sailors on, I could have traded one of my hands with someone whose hand was a silver hook. Think how dashing I'd look like that."

Nicholas quirks a fond smile at his sister. "I don't think sailors play at magic tricks with stowaways. I think they just throw them overboard."

"Oh." Kelsie purses her lips in a pout and sighs. "Perhaps it's best we have this boat instead, then."

Del teaches Nicholas some simple tricks, making

colours dance in the air and sparks dance from fingertip to fingertip. They make Kelsie's hair twist up into tightly coiled ringlets around her face, which makes her clap her hands in delight.

As evening falls, they drag the dory up onto the beach of the closest island, a small patch of land with nothing on it except a couple of rocks and some scrubby, pale-blue grass with a texture like old hay.

"We could try fishing again," Kelsie says doubtfully, spreading out the meagre remains of their edible supplies.

"Here, let me—" Del starts, touching a hand to Nicholas's elbow, guiding the other boy's arm in a series of movements. "Curl your fingers. Now straighten the thumb... there!"

The rather forlorn looking and extremely squashed bread roll in Kelsie's collection swells up as if inflated, to the size of a full loaf. The handful of bite-sized chunks of cheese begins to multiply, the pile growing to twenty and then thirty and then forty pieces, spilling upward and outward.

"There. It's magic food, though— you'll feel full, but your body's only getting fuel from that original little bun and those few bits of cheese. So we'll have to find proper food tomorrow, or start feeling weak," Del warns.

The twins nod in unison, which makes them all laugh a little, in the way it's only possible to laugh when you've been outdoors all day and there's lots of food to eat at the end of it.

When they've eaten their fill and their campfire is down to a warm steady glow, Del gets out his dice and starts to play again, until Nicholas grumbles that if Del's going to play stupid games, at least it should be a stupid game they can all play. So Del puts away his dice and Kelsie takes out the deck of cards instead, and they play stupid games like Go Fish and Snap and Black Maria until, during one particularly exuberant round of Snap, Nicholas's hand lands awkwardly on the Jack of Clubs and bends it in half.

A crease in one card makes the whole deck essentially

useless, so they give up on games and settle down for sleep.

Del wakes up first, his hair a heavy tangle around his head and neck. He hasn't bothered to cut it since this adventure began, so it's still long from his brief time as a girl at Kelsie's school.

Yawning, he sits up, scrabbling in his bag for the mirror he'd had hanging from a peg in his old cellar room, and the kitchen scissors he'd stuffed in as an afterthought during his escape. They stick a little as he gives them a tentative open and close, but it's not like he's trying to give himself the latest high-fashion style— he just wants the stupid hair gone.

The early-morning light has made the sea silvery, almost too bright to look at, and the sky is a more muted, less vivid blue than it was the day before. Del hopes the sunshine holds; he doesn't relish the idea of being stuck in a boat in the rain. Perhaps they'll make it to one of the bigger islands today and can go exploring.

He knows that this isn't much of a temporary solution, let alone one for the longer term. They'll have to decide where they want to go, if indeed the twins still intend to stay permanently run away.

He tells himself he doesn't care what they decide. It makes no difference to him at all. It's just that he'd rather know what their plans are before he makes his own— being on the run as a single youth will entail very different strategies to if there are three of them together. But he doesn't care. He'll be fine either way. He doesn't care.

"You look like a scarecrow," Kelsie says, walking around him to appraise the half-done haircut from different angles. "Here, give me those."

She takes the scissors and starts to snip away, evening out the wild tufts of Del's own attempt. "These scissors are awf... are these the kitchen scissors?"

"Um, yes?" Del asks, hoping the answer doesn't incur her wrath but suspecting that it will.

Kelsie just gives one of the most put-upon sighs Del

has ever heard, and goes back to cutting. "Hopeless," she declares. Then, reaching the grey streak in Del's hair, she gives an interested hum. "This bit has a different texture."

"Yes," Del agrees.

"I like it. It's nice." Kelsie snips the lock as short as those around it, keeping the cut-away piece in her hand. "I'm going to put it in my locket."

"But—" Del starts to protest, but then gives up with a slump of his shoulders. "All right. Fine. Put me in your mourning locket even though I'm still alive, along with your brother who is *also* still alive."

"Aaaand?" Kelsie prompts in an arch voice.

"And thank you for the haircut," Del adds, scruffing his hand over his trimmed hair. "I feel much more like me, now."

"Well, you look less like a scarecrow than you might have, so it'll do," she says decisively.

Even though the day isn't sunny, it's still bright enough to burn the twins' fair skin. Del, despite not being any darker-complected, doesn't have any trouble— years of outdoor work has left him much less sensitive. But Kelsie and Nicholas turn pink beneath their freckles rather quickly.

The colour makes Nicholas look healthier than before, gives him back a bit of the life drained away by the teacher at his school. Even though Del knows it's not real, just a trick of the sunburn, it's still nice to see, especially coupled with the happy grin that messing about with the sail and steering and his fishing line has given Nicholas. Maybe it's being around so much water that's making Del feel so charitable towards Nicholas; it makes him remember the village fountain and that autumn.

They pull up onto the shore of another, larger island at midday, when the sunlight on the water gets too much to bear. Dark, moss-covered ruins are visible through the undergrowth.

"It smells like dark magic here," Del warns. "Be careful.

Anything we find here is probably cursed."

"I thought you said magic wasn't intrinsically anything," Kelsie reminds him. Del shrugs.

"Well, it's not a *nice* place, how's that? Magic's been used for something terrible here."

If anything, that just makes Nicholas even keener to explore, and he leads the way to the half-collapsed temple through the foliage. Kelsie and Del trail behind, far less enthusiastically.

As well as the moss, the heavy granite slabs that serve as bricks on the old building are slick with seeping water and tangled vines, the latter dotted with a few lurid blooms despite the wintry season. Kelsie, usually so drawn to pretty things, makes no move to pluck any of the flowers. The occasional broken place on the plants oozes sap the colour of rotten blood.

"Stop shivering, you're both acting like children going through their first haunted house," Nicholas says scornfully, cutting a space in the doorway and pushing through into the interior. "This is no different from that church with the shuck, and you were eager enough to go in there."

"You don't understand," Kelsie argues, even as she pushes her way in after her brother. "You can't feel a sense of places like we can. This place isn't friendly at all. It doesn't want us here."

That just makes Nicholas laugh. "You can't expect to be welcome in every ruin you desecrate, can you?"

The corridor is wide but dark, with nothing but the light behind them and a similar rectangle of light in front of them to see by. There are animal bones here and there, mottled with mould or coiled with more vines.

At one point there's a scatter of tiny thorn-like darts on the ground, and more bones, and a few of the same little needles stuck in the cracks between the bricks on one side of the corridor.

"Careful," Nicholas says when Kelsie leans in for a closer look. "Those're obviously part of a trap. I bet they're poisoned."

"The trap has obviously been tripped already. Stop *fretting*."

Kelsie picks up one of the darts carefully, pinching the blunt end between her thumb and forefinger. She pulls the letter Nicholas posted to her when they were both still at school out of her satchel, and folds the dart inside it before slipping the whole thing into her little suede pouch.

"To help you remember the different places we went, since you're so terrible at it," she explains to Del.

Eventually the corridor widens out into a central atrium, which is lit with a greenish light by a wide skylight directly overhead. The sunshine filters down through a cover of leaves.

In the middle of this circular space is a wide well, the edges coming up to hip-height on the three new intruders. There's no sign of a winch or a bucket for drawing the water up, but when Del looks down into the depths he can see a faint, malevolent gleam far below, like distant black glass. He shudders, drawing back from the edge of the well. He has a creeping feeling at the back of his neck, as if they're being watched.

Nicholas is staring at the three blackened poles of wood off towards the edge of the room, where less light can reach.

Kelsie's looking at them too but from a distance, clearly more aware of what they are.

"People were burned here, weren't they?" Nicholas asks.

Del blinks. Turns out that Nicholas knows just as well as his sister. He's just incapable of feeling the terrible despair imprinted deeply into the charred stakes. Or perhaps he does feel it, but doesn't care. Del can only imagine how pitiless someone might become to the pain of others, after surviving torture of their own. Nicholas may have hardened his heart in self-defence.

"That's why there's a well here, too," replies Del. "To throw witches and wizards in, to see if they floated or not. If they drowned, they were innocent. If they survived, they were burned.

"The irony is that divination by water is itself a kind of magic. It's called hydromancy," Del says. "Water is one of the most powerful mediums spellcasters can use. They can even talk to one another over long distance with it, if they're good enough. That's called scrying."

He hesitates, and then— driven by the desolation of the place, perhaps— he says, "that's how I found out your step-father was going to sell me. I overheard a scrying conversation."

"Don't call him that," objects Kelsie. "You know we were always just afterthoughts to him."

Better cared-for afterthoughts then I was, he doesn't say, because what would be the point in saying it. It's not fair, really. They didn't really have any way of knowing what his life was like when he wasn't playing cards and kites with them.

The green light coming down through the roof begins to fade, and a rumble of thunder echoes hollowly around the expansive space.

"What a charming way to end this outing," Nicholas says in a dry voice, as if it's not largely his fault that they're in this awful place to start with.

Logically, the best thing to do is to stay in one of the under-cover parts of the temple until the rain subsides. They don't even discuss that as an option, though. The thought of staying in the grey half-dark and the cold, listening to the patter and hiss of the downpour hitting the water at the bottom of the well, is something none of them have any intention of entertaining.

So, with their hair plastered down and clothes dripping, they make their way back out through the undergrowth to the boat. The pebbly sand, gone as colourless as the sky, makes gritty crunches under the soles of their damp shoes.

"We could turn the boat over," suggests Nicholas. "Fold the sail down and roll the whole thing. Use it like a turtle shell over our heads."

"All right," Del and Kelsie agree, shoving their sodden sleeves up to their elbows and stepping in to help.

It isn't cosy inside the makeshift little cave. They're all too chilled and uncomfortable from their trek back through the wet jungle. The rain is too loud against the bottom of the dory, and the flat floor means they have to crouch down awkwardly to fit between it and the sand.

"It's not really so bad, though," Kelsie insists, determined to shake off the lingering grimness from the temple as quickly as possible. "I mean, we have food if we get hungry, and matches or flint or magic if it gets dark and we're still under here, and– oh!"

The last is a shout of surprise, as the dory is wrenched away from above them by a wave so huge and fast that it feels to Del like they've been struck by a rampaging monster as big as a house. It knocks them all apart like toys, throwing Nicholas and the dory in one direction, and Del in another, and Kelsie out into the choppy waves of the sea.

Del runs to the edge of the water and throws out a long rope of light, ignoring the resultant nosebleed as he tries to get it out to where Kelsie's intermittently visible in the violent grey water. She manages to grab it, winding it around her hands as he starts to pull her in.

"*Look!*" Nicholas shouts over the howling wind, pointing out to the horizon.

It's a tornado, or at least something very like one, a whirling coil of darkness twisting up and up impossibly high above the water, whipping waves and debris in all directions, coming for them at an alarmingly fast pace.

Del can feel his throat vibrating and realises he's letting out a dull moan of horror, the sound lost entirely beneath the din of the gale. His gaze snaps from the looming whirlwind to the golden rope stretching in a glowing line of light between himself and Kelsie... the *magic* rope that is *touching the waves* as she uses it to pull herself in, gulping and flailing, towards the beach.

Panicked, Del makes the rope vanish completely with a sharp flick of his hand. It's a little spell, smaller than the conjuring of the same rope just a minute before, but the immediacy with which Del demands it is enough of a blow to his body that he feels another warm trickle of wetness from his nose join the rain and seawater already drenching his face and choking him every time he opens his mouth to breathe.

Kelsie flounders at the sudden loss of the rope, losing her footing, but she's close enough to the shore that she soon rights herself and staggers up to the beach. She joins them as Del reaches Nicholas over near the remains of the dory, which is cracked along one side and missing half its mast.

"You have to run!" Del screams at them both. "This is all my fault! Run back into the jungle, into the ruins! Stay there until morn—"

"No!" Kelsie yells back. The tornado has nearly reached the island, and hearing anything over the shattering cacophony of destruction all around them is almost impossible.

He wants to shake her, to scream that this is a magical storm, that they have no hope of fighting back against what's bearing down on them. But, looking at their white, wide-eyed faces, Del knows that he doesn't need to tell them. They know all that already, and yet Kelsie at least is determined not to leave his side.

The Coral Sorcerer must have seen them through the well. That sense Del had of being watched, the predatory gleam of the dark water, hadn't just been his reaction to the pervading eeriness of the place.

Out of the whirl of wind and rubble, a hand as wide as the dory's broken sail reaches out, made of nothing but long thin shards of broken coral caught up in the whirlwind. It stretches towards them, the fingers curling out in claws made of a thousand little razors.

Del wants to run away even though he knows it's

useless. He wants to keep fighting for as long as he can, to make a break for it and go down fighting. But his feet and legs have gone sluggish with fear, rooting him to the spot as he stares up at the spindly fingers reaching out to grab him and pull him into the whirling void.

Suddenly Nicholas is there, between Del and that skeletal hand, and the other boy screams in pain as the fingers grasp around his wrist and tug him forward, hard enough to pull Nicholas's shoulder from its socket. Del feels an echo of the pain in his own hand, and realises it's the right— *his* right, Del's right, the hand Nicholas still wears from their swap— that has been caught and sliced to ribbons and pulled into the dark.

A split-second later, the hand and Nicholas and the queasy twisting blackness are all gone, sucked up into a single point and vanishing like water down a drain. There's nothing but Kelsie and Del and a raging ocean storm whipping sand and salt and ice into their faces as they try to cower from it.

Then the storm is gone too, and the world goes still in its aftermath.

A jagged shard of shell, thin and brittle as bone china, is embedded in Kelsie's cheek an inch below her eye. Del holds her face steady as he pinches the visible edge of the splinter and pulls it free, sending a rivulet of blood trailing down her cheek. Fat red droplets fall from her chin onto her clothes.

"Here, wait, let me—" he says, brushing his thumb over the wound and healing it with a quick spell. The effort is too much for his weary reserves of energy and his nose begins to bleed. He's not sure if it's ever stopped at all throughout all this.

They're both a gory, panicked mess, sand-grazed and soaked to the bone with freezing water.

"The boat's ruined," is the first thing Kelsie says. "Nicky will be so cross." Her voice cracks on her brother's name, but she manages to make it to the end of the sentence without breaking down, and instead of crying she sets her face in a determined expression. "Right. What do we do now?"

"I'll be able to find him. He's still got one of my hands, remember?" Del holds up his right palm, Nicholas's palm, and waves the fingers at Kelsie. "We can use me like a dowsing rod."

Kelsie bites her lip and blinks several times. "He can't even dowse," she mutters to herself. She twists her hands together, her fingers white from the pressure against each other. She looks at Del again, panicked. "What if the Coral Sorcerer realises that Nicky's not magical at all? What will happen?"

Del shakes his head. "It's all right. Not everything is about aptitude. The things... the things the Coral Sorcerer probably wants to use Nick for don't need it."

Kelsie goes white and presses her lips together hard, but she doesn't cry. She stares down at her feet, and wipes at the streak of blood on her cheek with her knuckles, and doesn't cry.

"I'm sorry," says Del. "It was stupid of me not to realise that the Coral Sorcerer saw us back at the well. I'm sorry I got you both caught up in all this."

Her gaze whips up to meet his own. "We got you caught up in our business too. Stop feeling sorry for yourself and start thinking about where we need to start looking."

Del rubs his thumb over the palm of Nicholas's hand. "The Coral Sorcerer has a secret entrance to his house. In the city. I know that much. Nobody knows where his real house is. Even your step-father doesn't—"

"*Stop calling him that*," Kelsie snaps.

"The Ruby Warlock doesn't know," Del corrects himself. They have more important things to do than argue about semantics.

"So it could be anywhere in the world," Kelsie says, despair edging into hysteria in her voice. "We can't search the whole *world*."

"We don't need to, though. Like I said, he's got an entrance to it in the city. A trapdoor, he called it. We can search a *city*."

Kelsie closes her eyes and takes a deep breath. "Yes. Yes, you're right. We can do that. How will we get there, though? The boat's ruined, and the city's miles and miles and miles down the river from the seashore anyway."

Del sends a high, urgent whistle into the air, breaking through the eerie calm which has settled over the storm-ravaged island in the hurricane's wake. A seagull with one leg and scruffy, grey-white feathers alights on the sand in front of them a few minutes later, pecking at the driftwood and seaweed scattered across the sand in search of food.

A wave of Del's hand and he and Kelsie are shrunk down to the size of doll house citizens, unsteady on their feet for a moment as they readjust to the new way gravity feels at this small size. They climb up onto the seagull's grubby back. Del whistles again and Kelsie yelps in surprise at the sudden hard rush of air as the bird flaps off up into the air and over the water.

The little boat becomes a tiny blue speck below and then vanishes off the horizon behind them, more ruins on the little islands for future explorers to find, a new salvage.

"We should try to get some sleep," Kelsie says hollowly, but neither of them make any move to try. They just sit together in silence, and wait for the seagull to take them where they're going.

The city is still a smudge on the horizon when Kelsie breaks the long silence, shifting restlessly and sighing loudly to herself.

"What?" Del finally asks.

"Do you think less of me? For killing him? The teacher, I mean. I haven't killed anybody else."

Del doesn't know what she wants him to say. Shifting around to look at her face doesn't give him any clues; her only expression is expectant, as she waits for him to answer.

After a few long moments of indecision, he shrugs.

"What?" Kelsie looks annoyed. "It's not a hard question."

"I don't know what answer you want."

"I want you to tell me the truth, of course. That's all I've ever wanted from you. Do you think what I did was wrong? Do you think less of me?"

Del thinks about her question. "It's hard to consider life to have some intrinsic value," he tells her carefully. "When your step... when my owner sold me off like farm machinery the moment I wasn't wanted. So, no. I don't suppose I think any less of you. It was loyal and brave to save your brother like that."

"I would have done it for you," says Kelsie. "If you'd told me what was happening."

Del knows it would hurt her if he says it never occurred to him at all to ask for help from her.

"There wouldn't have been time," he says instead. "And anyway, it's all past now."

"Yes," Kelsie agrees. Her voice sounds sad. Then she shakes herself out of it, and asks "Have you turned from boy to girl very often, before this adventure? Have you ever had reason to?"

"A few times. I don't remember which one I started as, but sometimes a spell needed one or the other in particular to be the caster, and I'd have to swap," Del replies. "Your step-fa... the Ruby Warlock had me as a boy most of the time— he said it was more convenient for most social hierarchies for me to be male. Not that I ever went much of anywhere. Maybe he just kept me that way because he wanted a boy apprentice instead of a girl one. Who knows?"

"It might have been mother's doing, once she was in the picture. She'd never have any girl servants on staff when my father was alive," Kelsie says. "That's why Nicholas and I started at our boarding schools in the first place, so she wouldn't have to hire a governess for us. She never would have stood for her husband having a girl assistant, no matter what the circumstances."

"What a horrible marriage they must have," remarks

Del. He's never thought about it before, but now it seems a fact that's impossible to miss.

"Yes," Kelsie agrees. "Spending the rest of your life— or even just the rest of their life, if you out-live them, I suppose— with somebody you don't trust? Eugh." She shakes her head. "Anyway. You really don't remember which one you were to start with? But don't you just sort of... of *know*?"

Del shrugs. "They feel about the same to me. I'm just more used to being a boy, so I choose that."

"What, really?" Kelsie looks puzzled. "But you must feel like one fits you and the other doesn't. I didn't feel at all *correct* when you transformed me into a boy version of myself. I don't imagine Nicholas would be any more comfortable than that with being a girl. Being one or the other is part of what makes somebody who they *are*."

There doesn't seem any way to respond to her confusion than with another helpless shrug. "Maybe for most people. Not for me. I'm both of them, or maybe neither."

Kelsie gives him a long, thoughtful look, then nods. "That must be part of what make you who *you* are, I suppose."

Del whistles to the seagull again as they reach the city's outskirts requesting that the bird take them somewhere that they'll be able to sleep. It alights on the roof of a dilapidated townhouse in a stinking, narrow street. The property is clearly not currently inhabited.

Unshrinking them back to normal size, and feeding the bird a handful of bread and cheese as a thank-you, Del takes stock of their surroundings as Kelsie sets about unsticking the water-warped window to the attic.

They seem quite close to the centre of town as far as Del can judge. The thick smoke of a thousand coal fires and factories makes it impossible to see very far in any direction.

"Got it," Kelsie says, and disappears inside. Del scatters the last few pieces of bread and cheese onto the rooftop for the bird and then follows her, letting the window swing shut behind him.

The attic of the townhouse is much colder and more decrepit than Del's old cellar room ever got even in the worst of winters. The roof slants sharply down to the floor at the edges of the space, and all the exposed beams are splintering and mildewed.

Kelsie looks around at the decay and dust of their new lodgings with the same numb stare that Del knows his own face often retreats to. It's the look of somebody who can't bear to feel the way they're feeling, and has decided that they're going to feel nothing at all instead.

"I need to get to work," she says, tone as carefully blank as her expression. "And so do you. I'm going to go down into the streets and start chatting to people. See if I can find anything out. You go flying; see if you can sense anything from the hand Nicky's still got of yours. We'll meet back here at midnight."

She doesn't change her clothes out of the torn and stained rags that the storm left her wearing, or try to brush her hair. The appearance of poverty will lend her an anonymity in a place like this. With a final nod goodbye, Kelsie goes down the stairs to the street level of the empty townhouse, and out into the street.

There's no need for Del to open the attic window again, since one of the panes of filthy glass is already mostly missing, with a few triangular shards of glass around the edges like a mouthful of broken, rot-jagged teeth. The wind blows through the hole with a haunted, hollow sound that's more like a pained moan than anything else.

In the city, most birds bigger than sparrow-size are either crows or pigeons. Maybe he's a bit of a snob, but Del can't imagine himself becoming a pigeon voluntarily, so he decides to be a crow instead. He transforms and hops out through the broken pane of the window, taking flight over the rooftops and chimneys of the city with a happy cawing cry.

It's beautiful up here, even if he's not as accustomed to the way the world looks through bird-eyes as he is with how the same sights look to people-eyes. There is room to move, to spread his wings and dip and cruise and dive at tasty-looking rubbish, to flit between steeples and chase the sharp angles of roofs and awnings.

It would be so easy to just lose himself to this, to forget about Kelsie and Nicholas and about being Del the runaway apprentice, and to just live the rest of his life as a crow up here on the upper edges and corners of the city's jumbled silhouette.

No, some part of him that's still a boy scolds the rest of him. *You can't. Not while Kelsie is somewhere down there in all those buildings and cobblestone streets.*

You can't, not while Nicholas is alone and afraid, stolen when it was really you that the thief was after.

Flying loses much of its charm at the thought of the twins. Crows, like so many kinds of bird, gravitate together into flocks. There's even a special name for when it's crows, Del thinks, but he can't remember what it is— his bird-brain is smaller than his person-brain, and doesn't have any use for the same sorts of labels and distinctions that people put onto things. A flock is a flock is a flock, whatever other titles it might wear as well. And Nicholas is part of Del's flock, and they need to get him back.

Birds have no sense of obligation or of grudging association or any of the other complicated names that Del and Nicholas might use for their connection to one another. As far as Del's crow-mind is concerned, there are simply birds that are yours and birds that are not, and Nicholas is one of the birds that is Del's. Or rather, one of the people. The whole matter of being a bird and a boy all at once is a little too conceptual for Del to easily deal with, so he decides to forgo the existential self-examination until he's back to being his usual person-self, and instead concentrates for now on not crashing into chimneys.

The search proves futile, for the time being, and when

the night gets cold enough to hurt, Del gives up on being a bird and lands back in the neighbourhood where he started. Shifting back into a boy (and gratefully noticing that he manages it without an attendant nosebleed), Del goes into a bakery and buys pies and buns with sausages for himself and Kelsie. They can't keep relying on magically augmented food, especially not if their coming days of searching are going to be anywhere near as exhausting as this one has been.

He carries the fragrant loot back to their temporary home, up through the crumbling shell of the lower levels to the attic. Kelsie's there already.

"You gave up early, too?" she asks, voice a weary croak.

"Don't think of it as giving up," Del replies, handing over half the food. "We're saving our strength for a proper look tomorrow."

"Mm," Kelsie says around a mouthful of pie. "I never thought I'd be so grateful for something as disgusting as this."

"Yes, they're surprisingly nice, aren't they? So long as you don't think too much about it," Del agrees, munching on a sausage wrapped in a slice of bread. "Do you remember what a flock of crows is called?"

Kelsie snorts. "Of course I do. It's a murder. Everyone knows *that*, because it's so dramatic."

"Oh, right. I forgot," confesses Del.

"You have the most awful memory, honestly." Kelsie shakes her head in despair.

"Speaking of memory," says Del. "You remembered not to use your real name, didn't you?"

Kelsie snorts. "Yes. I am actually stupid enough to do that. You're right."

"I was just checking," Del snipes back. "If I'd really been worried about it, I'd've asked you beforehand, wouldn't I?"

"Oh no, you don't fool me. You didn't even think of it until just now, because it isn't something you ever worry about. You only ever have to be yourself."

"That's not true," says Del. "I wasn't always myself. Well, I was. But I decided what I was called. The Ruby Warlock wanted me to be named Gilfaethwy."

Kelsie looks at him expectantly.

"What?" Del asks.

"You can't just leave it at that. Tell me the rest of the story!"

"Oh." The memory makes his mouth twitch in a smile. "Well. It turned out that the Ruby Warlock couldn't be bothered to yell 'Gilfaethwy!' whenever I was needed. And really, I was too small for such a big name.

"So he ended up just calling me 'child' whenever he needed me to do something. And that was the only time he spoke to me; he didn't bother to give me any other name. When I was five years old, I decided to name myself. I picked out 'Del.'"

He holds his hands out in a 'there you go' gesture.

Kelsie's expression is deeply sad. "Nicky and I used to spend lots of our time being wretchedly self-pitying at each other, because we knew our mother didn't really love us. But she always did right by us, even if it was just out of duty. She wasn't ever... we shouldn't have complained."

Del rolls his eyes. "That's not how it works. You should be clever enough to know that. Just because somebody else is more miserable than you are doesn't mean you can't be miserable too. That's like saying that just because somebody's got an even happier life than you, then you shouldn't be happy about the one you've got. You see?"

"All right, all right, clever clogs. I'm clever enough that I didn't say my name was Kelsie, and that's plenty smart enough for our current purposes. We can leave the philosophy lessons for after we get Nicky back."

"What name did you give yourself?"

Kelsie shrugs one shoulder. "Octavia. It's the most common name you can get, for our age and younger. There were thirteen of them just at my school."

"Really? That's surprising."

"It's because of Princess Aria. She was the littlest, the seventh baby in the royal family and the one who died last of all out of all of them— she was really Queen Aria at the end, I suppose, since the King and Queen had been killed already. Then she got killed too, of course.

"There were all sorts of rumors and stories that she'd been saved from it, smuggled out of the palace in a tinker's cart and given to a lost infant's home to raise. People love a good mystery, even if it's really just a stupid conspiracy theory. The rebels had killed six babies already, why would they let the last one get away like that?

"Anyway, that's why people started naming their girl babies Octavia. It was a way to show that they still recognized Aria as their proper Queen, you see? You only get an eight-name if you believe seven is still alive."

Del feels unnerved by the topic, and frowns. "That's awful. Why don't they just call babies Aria, instead?"

Kelsie shrugs. "Don't ask me why people think the way they think! If they ever made the slightest bit of sense, I would be so shocked I'd fall over dead right then and there.

"Anyway, her name wasn't really Aria. That was just her nickname. Her real name was Rowan Septima Cainwen something something."

Del flinches at the name but Kelsie doesn't notice.

"I forget what the last ones were. I guess her parents felt the same way you did— babies are too little for big names. 'Aria' is the proper name of the Whitebeam tree— the white rowan. Everyone who saw her commented on how white her hair was. It was like fairytale-princess hair. Though I suppose fairytale princesses have happier endings than she did."

Del clamps down hard on the roiling panic the story has stirred up in him and attempts a smirk. "You haven't read that many fairy tales, if you think that."

A little while later, as they explore the room, Kelsie points over to a far corner. "What's that over there? It looks like it might be something terrible and awful."

"So naturally you want to investigate it," Del observes dryly. "I'm so glad I'm on a perilous rescue mission with someone morbid. Really." He walks over to investigate the discovery . "It's some very dead rats. Just their bones. Does that count as terrible and sad?"

Kelsie joins him. "It's not just that. I think it's the bones of a rat king," she says. There's no fear in her tone, or even disgust. Just fascination.

"I've never seen one, just sketches in books," Del says, crouching beside her so he can get a better look. There really is hardly anything left but bones— the flesh and fur is just thick dust. The tails are like tiny spines or the knucklebones of long, spidery, many-jointed fingers. There are six skeletons, and the knot binding their ends of their tails into a clump is matted with tangled pink thread.

"I didn't know for sure if they were real, or just made up for stories," says Kelsie. "Look at the yarn there. They must have knocked over a spindle, or unravelled a shawl trying to get at something underneath. Just a little accident, and it stuck them all together for the rest of their lives."

"I don't know that they'd be able to live at all. That's probably why rat kings are so rare; when they happen the rats just sneak off into a hole and die and nobody finds them."

Kelsie shakes her head. "No. Look at the tails in the knot." She reaches out without a hint of squeamishness and plucks one of the tiny knuckle-pieces of bone out of the grimy dust. It's creamy-white, like old ivory, and slightly crooked at one end. "See? It's bent. That means the rat wasn't completely grown-up when it became part of the rat king. The bone kept growing inside the knot, where it grew crooked to fit into its spot in the tangle."

Del can feel his eyes go wide. Every so often, Kelsie will say or do something which reminds him just how clever she is.

"You would have made an excellent witch," he tells her.

She shrugs, resting the bone in her palm as she

continues to examine it, as Del has sometimes seen her mother examine jewels or flowers. They have similar faces, though in Del's opinion Kelsie is the more beautiful of the two. Not because of anything in particular about her features— it's the expressions which play lightning-fast across Kelsie's face as her brain evaluates and considers the world around her which gives her such life and loveliness.

"I still might," she says, giving him a disbelieving smile. "Once we've got Nicky back, you can teach me properly."

It's not until that moment that Del understands that, for all Kelsie's optimism, she doesn't expect to make it out of this alive any more than he does.

Still... the rat king lived despite its tangles. Perhaps their bones will have a chance to grow. Del's certainly seen stranger things occur.

A spark of optimism kindles in his chest.

"I will," he tells her, determined to restore her faith. Even if they do end up dying, at least Del can make sure that Kelsie has hope against that outcome in the meantime. "We might even get a spark or two out of your useless brother."

She laughs quietly and leans against him. It's companionable there, down amongst the bones and dust.

After midnight, when the world is dark and still and endless, Del hears Kelsie's breathing change and knows that she's awake beside him. He doesn't sleep very much. He's not used to having another person in the bed beside him.

"Kelsie," he whispers. She gives a soft hum in reply. "Do you think the rats in the rat king hated each other, or liked each other?"

She hums again, thoughtful this time, and shifts around a little under the blankets. "Doesn't really matter, does it?" she answers him, her voice sleepy. "They were bound together either way."

In the morning, Kelsie takes Del out to show him what she managed to find out the day before. This early, barely past dawn, the air is even colder than it was in Del's little garden at the same hour. The pair of them walk as fast as the slippery cobblestones underfoot allow, talking so their teeth won't chatter. The white streak of Del's hair, never easy to tame, keeps blowing forward and tickling his face.

"That corner there, outside the bookstore? There's a man who stands and whispers to the people going past that he's got special tracts for sale, sealed up in envelopes, going extra-cheap and only a couple of pennies each.

"Of course, everybody thinks they're dirty stories, so they pay the money and hurry off with the envelopes stuffed inside their coats like secrets. But he likes me, so he opened one up to show me what's inside. It's those pamphlets that church volunteers give out to prostitutes, all about how the wages of sin are hellfire and that nonsense."

"Because nobody's ever going to come back to beat the stuffing out of him for that, I'm sure," notes Del.

Kelsie giggles. "He says he moves around enough that nobody can ever find him."

"Sounds exhausting." Del's already weary with life on the run, and it's really not so long at all since he packed up all his things and became a bird to find her. He can't imagine what it would be like to stay that way forever, only a step or two ahead of danger and always moving forward.

It might be that this is what awaits him, if he survives. Once the twins are gone their own way. The thought makes him sad.

"And that shop on the corner there sells spectacles and magnifying glasses and glass eyes," Kelsie says, nodding at a large front window with various lenses and frames on display against a blue felt backdrop. "Maids with strange eyes can't get work, not easily. They're supposed to be a bad omen. Seems like everything on earth's a bad omen, if you listen to superstition." She sighs, then shrugs. "I don't know if the same thing's said about apprentices. If it is, you'll have to get your eyes back from me. Mine'll never get you hired."

Del gives her a surprised look. "I'd completely forgotten that we did that," he laughs. He's so used to looking at her face that he's stopped even thinking about the fact that her eyes haven't always been the ice-pale blue that they are now. They're so familiar to him that it's very strange to remember that it's a borrowed shade she wears; that those are really Del's own irises he sees when he stares at her.

"Do you want to switch back?" he asks, strangely afraid that she'll say yes. But all Kelsie does is bump her shoulder against his and shake her head.

"Of course not, stupid. Neither of us are maids, are we? And who knows, with the luck we're having lately, we might need the connection to find one another, like Nicky's hand is going to help us find him."

There's a boy with a little folding table, shuffling three cards in a complicated dance around each other on the small surface. Kelsie slows down to watch, and the boy grins at them both.

"Mornin'."

"It's like a shell game," answers Kelsie. "Isn't it?"

The boy, whose face is shadowed and pinched from lack of sleep and food but whose eyes are big and brown and pretty, nods. "Just the same, only instead of three cups with a ball hidden under one I've got these fellows and their lady."

He turns the cards face-up, showing them the Jack of Spades, the Jack of Clubs, and the Queen of Hearts. "Want a try?"

Kelsie shakes her head. "Sorry. I don't have the money to play."

"Oh, I wouldn't charge you for a game, love." The boy grins. He's young enough that one of his front teeth is still just beginning to grow in. "Couldn't start my day taking winnings off a fellow workin' soul like you. Be bad luck for me, wouldn't it?"

"What makes you so sure you'd win? Maybe I'd pick the right card. It doesn't look *that* hard."

"Ah, that's the beauty of it, ain't it? Everyone thinks they'll be smarter than the cards for sure. But trust me; nobody wins a round of this unless I want them to."

Kelsie laughs at the frank honesty in the boy's tone. "Is it magic, then? That makes you certain you'll always win?"

That causes the boy to make a scoffing sound and roll his eyes. "Nah. Magic, *that's* the real mug's game, if you ask me. No, alls I need is me cards and cleverness."

"Well, good luck," Kelsie says with a smile, bidding the boy farewell with a nod. Del falls into step beside her as they continue on their way.

"You never make conversation with anybody," Kelsie says to him. "Why not? You could have said hello to him. That's all I did, and I ended up making a friend."

"Children like that don't have friends," Del notes absently, distracted by the noise and colour of the rapidly crowding street around them. He doubts he'll ever feel at home in a city, not truly.

"You mean like *you*," Kelsie grumbles, but lets the matter drop.

Later, when they've parted ways to keep on searching, Del keeps going over Kelsie's words in his head. She might not be entirely incorrect.

He's reluctant to go straight into bird form and flying, anyway. All he's getting from the echo of his hand on Nicholas's wrist is pain, aching waves of hot tender pain. Not only will that be useless to navigate by, it's also quite distressing even second-hand.

Heh. Second-hand. Del will have to remember that pun, to irritate Nicholas with later. It's always worth holding onto particularly annoying things that he can say around the other boy.

In the interests of procrastinating his flight, Del decides to put Kelsie's theory of friendship to the test. He goes back to the bakery and buys another pie, this time taking it around to where the boy from that morning is still plying his three-card monte game.

There's nobody currently trying their skill at the rigged game, so Del approaches the boy and offers the pie. The boy bites it immediately, clearly too hungry for either skepticism or politeness.

"Do you know of any magicians who come around this area?" he asks, when the boy's had time to chew and swallow a few mouthfuls.

"Nah. Them toffs ain't got no time for this end of town," the boy says, shaking his head. "You want to speak to any of them, you're better going over that way." He points vaguely in a random direction. Del's pretty certain that the boy doesn't have any more idea of where to find a spellcaster in the city than Del himself does.

Oh well. Del nods his thanks for the advice, and leaves

the boy to his pie and his cards. Del's borrowed hand is hurting even more, and he worries that Nicholas may be dealing with a serious infection on top of all the other problems they've got.

On his way back to the attic he passes the glass eyes and spectacles shop. He dawdles by the window, trying to distract himself from the ache in his hand. The sight of the magnifying glasses on display makes him think of the Ruby Warlock, bent over spellbooks with a magnifier. Del remembers why he's never bothered to cultivate a good memory, as the thought of his old master gives him a bright hot hurt in his chest.

"You just gave that boy over there a pie, didn't you?" the store owner asks, coming out to stand on the step and speak to Del.

Del nods, warily.

"Yes. He's not hurting anyone, though."

The shopkeeper laughs gently. "I'm not angry at you. It was a kind thing to do. Look, that glass eye you've got there isn't a good shade at all. Nobody's ever had a green like that. You'll never get work while you're still using it. Here."

He hands Del a small, rather heavy little cloth bundle. "Because you gave that boy a pie, even when you and your sister clearly need what money you have."

Del thinks about correcting the man, telling him that Kelsie's not his sister, but there's no real reason to complicate things, to stop the man feeling so pleased about his own simple generosity. It's easier to smile and say, "Thank you, sir, thank you very much," and hurry back to the attic with the little bundle grasped in one hand while the other hand stings and stings from someone else's pain.

Back in the attic, Del gets his mirror out of his pouch again to examine his eyes. The man at the store was right. Nobody's eyes are as green as Kelsie's.

The brightness isn't so striking that most would notice how odd it is, not yet. But the man noticed, and Del can see it now.

Before he can wonder at it though, the pain in his right hand abruptly escalates to a level so bad that his knees give out from under him, and he sits down hard on the edge of the bed trying not to yell out from the agony of it.

And then, just as fast, the pain's gone completely, like a door slamming shut and cutting all the light out of a room. The absence is almost as bad as the pain, because in that moment Del knows that Nicholas has lost his hand, and with it their best chance of finding him is gone.

Del paces the room, trying to think of what they should do next. When Kelsie comes back to check in at midday, that's what she finds him doing, his hair a wild mess from where he's been running his hands through it as he thinks.

"You've been thinking about Nick particularly hard yesterday and today, haven't you?" he asks, not bothering to open with a hello.

Kelsie looks confused. "Well, yes, of course I have been."

"It must be because he's around so much magic. It's amplifying the connection you have," Del mutters to himself.

"What are you talking about? What's going on?"

Del stops pacing and looks at her. "Kelsie... I think Nicholas has lost his hand. I'm almost sure of it."

Her own hands fly to her mouth in horror and she looks at him with wide, horrified eyes. "Oh no," she manages to say. "Oh no, oh no."

"No, don't, it's all right," Del picks up the little wrapped bundle off the mattress. "The man at the glass eye store gave me this today, because he said that my own green eye would never pass for real."

Kelsie unwraps the bundle. She looks down at the glass eye nestled in her palm. "But you don't have a glass..." she says, then looks at Del's face again. "My eye's never been that green before. Why's it changed?"

"I think it's because Nick must be around a lot of magic at the Coral Sorcerer's house. It's amplifying the connection you have with him."

"Nicholas isn't magic, though," Kelsie objects, more confused by the minute. "There's not a drop of magic in him."

"*You're* his magical part. Your magic makes him magic. We can... I think, maybe, we can use that to find him. I've never seen two people so connected. I didn't know people could affect each other like you two affect each other."

"You never saw much love at all, did you?" Kelsie asks, tucking the eye into her pocket and sitting down on the bed. She sounds very tired.

"I was fine. Your stepfather was never a cruel man," Del says stiffly, feeling weirdly protective of the Ruby Warlock's reputation despite everything.

And Kelsie bursts into tears.

"Kel... Kelsie, what's... I don't understand, why are you crying?"

"I *know* you don't understand, I know, I *know*. That's *why I'm crying*," she sobs. "I'm crying because you don't know that there's anything to be sad about. You've never... I'm crying because my brother is in danger, and I'm crying because I'm *hungry* and I'm *tired* and I just want everything to be *all right* again, but it won't *ever* be, even if we get Nicholas back things can never be *anything* like they were, and everything, just *everything* is wrong."

Her weeping is hot and angry and dramatic as she speaks, but when her words are done it turns quieter, more desolate, and she sits with her face buried in her hands and cries and cries and cries.

Del feels awkward and clumsy and useless as he moves in close beside her, putting his arm around her shoulders and giving her a gentle hug. "No," he says. "Things can't be like they were. But we'll find a new way for them to be. I promise."

She doesn't say anything in reply, and eventually her tears trail off to silence. She takes a deep, ragged breath. "All right. So what do we do now?"

Since they don't really have any idea how to go about

answering that question, they go through the motions and do all that they can to prepare. They pack their bags, making sure to collect what food and other supplies they can. This whole fraught debacle has more than enough dangers, hardships and terrors in it without them overlooking practical considerations and being undone by something as basic as thirst or a lack of clean socks or something as prosaic as that.

When there's no way that they can justify more time spent packing and re-packing, they start off walking.

Every pungent, narrow laneway thronged with people; every mossy sunlit park adorned with winding paths. They skirt around the edges of enthusiastic, deafening games of Princess Aria, just as raucous and rambunctious no matter whether it's pampered, rosy-faced children in parks or grimy alley-urchins playing it among the rubbish bins and gutters.

Kelsie and Del walk until the sun goes down and then they walk until it comes up again.

The second day is even more useless than the first. It's difficult for something to be less satisfying than 'no leads,' but they manage it somehow: not only don't they find anything, again, but this time they're snappish and weary from no sleep, and disheartened from no progress.

"This is hopeless," Kelsie says eventually, sitting down on an upturned wheelbarrow regaled to a junk heap. "There's too much city to look through. By the time we even start to find the right path, it'll be..."

She trails off. Del isn't surprised. Even at her most defeated, Kelsie will never truly give up on her brother. It will never, ever be 'too late,' because failure is something she cannot even contemplate. To lose Nicholas is unthinkable.

Del learned long, long ago that unthinkable losses happen all the time, and the world never bothers to pause in its endless momentum just because something unfathomably terrible has happened to somebody somewhere.

The world won't end if Nicholas dies. But something important inside Kelsie will. And in Del, too.

"We'll find it," Del promises her, even though he knows his words may be a lie.

Far too depleted to walk any more, they curl up together against the oven-warm wall of a bakery and rest as best they can until morning.

On the evening of the third day, Del and Kelsie are almost too exhausted to feel exhausted anymore. It's not the walking that's making them weary, but rather the surprisingly large amount of energy it takes to sustain optimism and hope in the face of such dismaying circumstances.

Del already knew that the simple act of not giving up is sometimes the most difficult thing in the world, but it's clearly something Kelsie's never thought about before. And even the already-knowing that Del's got isn't any kind of advantage: he still has to work just as hard to keep on believing that there's any point at all to what they're doing.

"We don't even know what it's going to look like," he says, unable to stop his mood spilling over into his words. He's just *tired*. Maybe that's all defeat is; being too tired to keep trying. "We don't know if it's a seal or a mark or if it's *nothing*."

"Stop it," Kelsie snaps, sounding very like Del feels. "It's barely sunset. You can't be bored of this already."

The attempted flippancy in her choice of words falls flat. Neither of them have any energy left for true banter. Del scuffs his foot against the ground and feels hopeless.

"Sunset..." Kelsie says again, staring up at the sky above a small wrought-iron gate beside them. It's the kind of gate that leads from walled courtyards to wider gardens. Del stops, trying to see whatever it is that has made Kelsie pause.

Through the gate he can see a small, nicely kept flower patch, the sort that are scattered here and there throughout the city. What's different about this one is that the colour of the sky visible through the gate is just a fraction different from the colour of the sky over the city. The red of the sunset over the city is murkier, dirtier. Through the gate, the shade is as delicate and unsullied as coral.

"Kelsie," Del says, hardly daring to believe his eyes. "You *did* it."

"I told you not to give up, didn't I?" she says, but there's such relief in her voice that it doesn't come out as the retort she meant it to be. It just sounds like she's trying to believe her own eyes, too.

The gate is locked, of course, but Del has been a crow and a girl and Kelsie has been a sparrow and a boy, and they've survived hurricanes and looked at the blackened posts where people burned to death. No locked gate is going to stop them now.

Still, even as Del casts a spell to work the latch and open the trapdoor, he can hear the panic in Kelsie's breaths and see the uncertainty in her eyes. They don't know what's waiting for them beyond this threshold, and that uncertainty is more frightening than any concrete threat would be.

"It's just like bringing me the dinner tray," Del tells her. "All you have to do is act like you have every right to be wherever you are, and most people won't even think of stopping you. It's true for spells, as well. You just need to trick it into doing what you want."

She closes her eyes tight and nods. "O...okay. Let's go," Kelsie says, obviously trying hard to sound as confident as she can.

The passage on the other side of the door is too narrow for them to walk comfortably side-by-side, so Del takes the lead and they go as carefully and quickly and quietly as they can. There's a smell in the air that's sharp and cold, like snow.

After only a few minutes of walking, the passage breaks off in two directions. "You go this way," Kelsie orders Del, pointing at one of the options. "And I'll go that way."

"Do you really think that's a good idea, splitting up?"

She gives a derisive snort. "None of this has been a good idea. But we'll get out of here quicker if we can look over more ground."

"All right, but when you find yourself facing down the Coral Sorcerer all on your own, don't come crying to me," Del says, instead of goodbye. He notices that they're both making a rather pointed effort not to say goodbye, as they break off in the two directions.

After the first divide, Del's route through the passage becomes even more labyrinthine. He thinks of the long, straight passageway in the ruined temple, and how frightening and unwelcome that place had felt. The Coral Sorcerer's house carries no such foreboding in its architecture, and Del can't help but feel that this is unfair. The truly evil places of the world should not be so deceptively innocuous, and yet they are.

Ten, perhaps fifteen minutes after parting ways with Kelsie, Del reaches the dungeon.

There's no filthy stone floor, or even bars and heavily locked doors to keep the prisoner from escaping. Just a blank, rather ordinary looking room, with a key hanging on a nail hammered into the door frame. There was a nail and a key not so very different from these ones, on the door between the kitchen and the garden back at the Ruby Warlock's house. Weirdly, Del feels almost angry at the similarity; it doesn't seem right for a place like this to be able to taint those old small memories he has.

There are no bars or locked doors, so the key can't be for those, but it's obvious what needs to be unlocked. Nicholas is sitting on a thin, rather grubby-looking mattress pushed against the far corner of the room, and his one remaining hand is braceleted by a thick copper-coloured cuff that's chained to a bolt in the wall.

"Careful, there's a—" Nicholas starts to say as Del steps over towards him, only to be thrown back by a sharp, painful shock from an invisible barrier running down the centre of the room. "I *tried* to tell you."

"You could have tried *harder*," Del grumbles, standing up again. Tentatively, he steps forward, hand held out in front of him to gingerly feel out where the force field begins. When he finds it, the pain makes him pull back his hand, the fingertips stinging from the touch.

He tries again, forcing himself not to pull away immediately. It's like trying to keep his palm steady over a candle-flame, seeing how long he can endure it before he surrenders. Del pushes forward and forward, trying to see if the barrier is permeable apart from pain, or if it's solid in some other way as well.

It doesn't seem to be. All right. That's good. Pain is endurable. Pain can be ignored, if there's a good enough reason to ignore it.

"When I say 'go'," he says to Nicholas. "You shut your eyes and imagine that you have your hand back, all right? You have your hand back and there's a key in the palm of it."

Del collects the key off the nail and closes his fingers tight around it, then carefully feels his way back to the invisible place where the barrier begins. He takes a deep breath, and grits his teeth, and squeezes his eyes shut.

He forces himself to remember the storm on the beach and how fearlessly Nicholas had stepped in front of Del. The least Del can do now is try to repay that fearlessness in kind. He balls his hand— Nicholas's hand, really, Del was ever only borrowing it— into a tight fist around the key and punches forward, forcing himself not to cry out as the resistance of the barrier sends a shock of pain up his arm and through his shoulder.

"*Now,*" he chokes out.

It hurts. It hurts a lot. But what Del notices, even more than he notices the pain, is how *strange* it feels. His entire arm is tingling, like the worst case of pins and needles mixed with a badly jolted funny bone mixed with the overload of sensation that comes equally from very hot or very cold water.

He can still feel his hand. Intellectually, he knows it isn't there. He can even see it isn't there, just a sore red stump where his wrist used to give way to the heel of his palm. But no matter what his eyes and his brain tell him, he can still sense it there, numb and paralyzed but *present* on the mental map of himself.

Del wrenches his arm back through the barrier, holding it tight against his chest and trying to breathe through the overwhelming discomfort.

Nicholas opens the tightly-curled fingers of his newly restored hand. The edges of the key have cut red-and-white welts into the skin of his palm.

He's trembling, tears forming at the corners of his eyes from pain and exhaustion as he hauls himself up against the wall to a standing position and fumbles at the lock on the other hand's shackle. It opens with a begrudging creak from the metal and several grunts of effort from Nicholas. His wrist is marked with a ring of pressure sores from where he has rubbed and pulled like an animal in a trap, desperate to escape. He takes one shaky step, and then another.

"This is going to hurt," Del warns him as he approaches the barrier. Then Del blinks in surprise, shocked at the feeble sound of his own voice. Nicholas gives him a crooked, weary grin.

"Can't take a little sting?" he asks with raised brows, nodding at the truncated wrist cradled against the front of Del's shirt. "What kind of pathetic rescuer are you?"

"Just hurry up," croaks Del, exasperated already. He hasn't been ten minutes in Nicholas's company and he's sick of him all over again.

Nicholas rolls his shoulders, sets his gaze to middle-distance, and shoves through the barrier. Once he's through he collapses to his hands and knees, retching from the pain and shuddering. A trickle of thin, nasty-smelling bile comes out of his mouth, but nothing more than that—it's obvious that he hasn't eaten in days, perhaps since before the Coral Sorcerer took him.

"There's food in my bag," Del says. "But you'll have to get it out yourself. I won't be able to undo the knot I tied."

"Later," Nicholas says, standing up. "For all we know, you've set off a dozen alarms already. We should get out of here immediately."

Without discussing it, the two boys lean against one another for support as they begin to move back the way Del came, as fast as they're capable of walking.

"Good thing we're small," Del murmurs as they go. If either of them were any bigger, the pair of them probably wouldn't fit shoulder-to-shoulder in the narrow corridor.

"Maybe we can make our fortunes in the three-legged-race industry. Enclosed spaces division," Nicholas jokes in reply, the last few words chopped into syllables by a ragged bout of coughing that he can't shake until they stop for a few seconds and Del thumps him lightly between the shoulder blades with a flattened palm.

The flattened palm, really, since he's only got the one now.

Del hopes that the coughing hasn't given them away, but at this point he's fully aware that if they actually manage to get out without being found it will be nothing short of miraculous.

"Second thought, maybe not," Nicholas whispers when he's got his breath back. "We're pretty rubbish at making good time at it. Wouldn't be worth going into racing."

They stumble mostly in silence after that, all their concentration fixed on keeping their footing as even as quick as they're able.

"Kelsie's going to meet us back here," Del says when they finally approach the place where the tunnel divides into two.

"What's she doing?"

"Looking for you," Del answers. "Same as me. We thought we'd cover more ground if we split up."

"That's the worst strategy for anything I've ever heard,"

Nicholas says, looking genuinely aghast. "Have neither of you ever heard a ghost story in your lives? Splitting up is the quickest way to hand victory to the enemy on a silver platter. Very generous of you to do that."

"You're not very good at being rescued, did you know that?" says Del with a scowl.

"Well you're clearly not very good at rescuing, so I suppose it all balances," snipes Nicholas.

Time drags as they wait for Kelsie, with Nicholas very pointedly not saying 'I told you so' and Del just feeling anxious.

"Del?" the quiet call eventually sounds, just before Kelsie comes into view from around the bend in the passageway. She sees her brother and a moment later has launched herself at him, knocking them both back against the wall as he stumbles under her weight and momentum. A hefty rock she'd been holding in one hand clatters to the ground.

Del moves out of the way, to give them the reunion to themselves. He rests his back against the wall for a moment and closes his eyes, hoping that will help him from feeling so sick and dizzy. It doesn't, so he opens them again.

Nicholas and Kelsie are simply standing there, eyes closed, foreheads pressed together.

"I knew you'd find me," Nicholas says.

"Glad one of us was certain," replies Kelsie, her words catching on a sob. Then she blinks and pulls away from the embrace, taking a deep breath to steady herself and looking over at Del. "All right, we can have some more hugs later. This has all been much too easy—" She ignores Del's objecting scoff at that. "So we're probably inside a trap. Let's go be somewhere else before it closes, shall we? Are you both all right to run?"

"For a little while," Del answers with a nod, which Nicholas echoes with his own.

Soon the jagged energy which came with the pain of losing his hand will run out, as will the excitement of this whole ludicrous rescue attempt. When that happens, Del knows he'll be useless for anything. But for the time being, he can run.

"What's the rock for?" Nicholas asks her as they set off.

"I don't know." Kelsie hefts the stone in her hand. "I thought it might be good to have some sort of weapon."

"You were going to throw a rock at a wizard. That was your plan. To throw a rock."

"Or hit him! I don't know! I needed to have some kind of plan, didn't I?"

"Hopeless." Nicholas shakes his head. "Absolutely hopeless. I don't know how you managed even a day without me. Magic makes people forget how to be *sensible*."

"So what's your excuse, then?" Del counters. Nicholas glares at him.

Kelsie leads them back through the twisting maze of the rest of the passageways, back towards the trapdoor out into the city. The hallways seem to go on forever.

"Not far now," Nicholas says as they turn another corner.

"How would you even know?" Del snaps, momentarily invigorated by irritation at Nicholas's tone. A moment later he realises that's the point– Nicholas is attempting to *annoy* Del into staying upright and moving.

"Wait, shut up," Kelsie whispers to them both, freezing mid-step and holding up her hand to halt them both along with her.

Then Del hears it, the sound that made her stop. A footstep, not far behind them.

"Run," he says, fear turning his veins to ice as he wonders if he still has it in him to even try to get away.

Kelsie and Nicholas nod. Their footsteps aren't quiet now. All that matters is speed. Del struggles to keep pace with them.

And then an invisible punch smacks into him from behind, sending him sprawling on his knees.

He puts out his hands to break his fall, and as the half-healed stump of his wrist hits the tiled stone floor the pain is so bad that he's momentarily blinded by black and white stars across his vision.

He curls onto his side, whimpering and clutching at his arm; waves of nausea make him retch.

Somewhere, beyond the cage of pain he's trapped in, Del hears the footsteps draw near, and Nicholas's shout as the twins realise that Del is no longer just behind them.

Del forces his eyes open. Kelsie and Nicholas are staring and him, their mouths open in shock and dismay. A fresh wave of pain batters him as the Coral Sorcerer's foot kicks him between his shoulder blades, and he has to bite his tongue to keep back a scream.

"Run!" he chokes out again, squeezing his eyes shut. He can't bear to watch them escape without him. He'll survive whatever the Coral Sorcerer has in store for him; he'll be able to stand it, so long as he doesn't have the memory of Nicholas and Kelsie running out of sight.

The ground under him changes and he hears Kelsie scream, and when he opens his eyelids again it's to see that they're no longer in the corridors at all. They're in a library, all glossy dark wood and leather and shiny brass.

Nicholas and Kelsie are a little distance away from him, closer to the door, and judging by the heavy, quick kick that breaks one of Del's ribs a moment later, the Coral Sorcerer is just beside him.

"Get up," the Coral Sorcerer demands, and Del's arms and legs pull him to his feet without his participation. It's an incredibly unnerving feeling, to be manipulated like a child's jointed doll, and Del can't help the moan of fright that bubbles up his throat.

The moan turns to coughing and spluttering, as the ungentle movement of being pulled to standing jostles something torn inside his chest. Del coughs up a bright bloom of blood, splattering a gory smear across the floor. He can't help but hope that he's just ruined an expensive carpet; little victories are worth taking where they're found.

"You impertinent little whelps." The Coral Sorcerer sounds furious. Del still can't move much more than his mouth and eyes, and so is stuck frozen and watching helplessly as the Coral Sorcerer steps away from him and towards the twins. "I've half a mind to give you both a good beating before I send you back to your idiotic parents. How dare you make me go to such lengths to get back my rightful property?"

All the fight and bravado has drained out of the twins. They look like weary, grubby, terrified children, caught in something far beyond the edges of their world.

Del knows that he will miss them for the rest of his life, however long or short a time that proves to be.

"The only reason you got in at all," the Coral Sorcerer says to Kelsie, his voice a vicious hiss. "Was because it served my purposes for you to attempt to rescue your useless brother."

Del can tell that this much, at least, is a lie. He gives a ragged, thready laugh, smiling with bloodied teeth. "If that were true," he rasps. "You'd never have let us trade our hands back. Why damage your intended prize?"

He makes himself laugh again, even as the Coral Sorcerer strikes him hard across the face and sends him sprawling to the ground again. It's the least laughter-like, most terrible sound Del's ever heard anybody make, but now that he's started he can't stop. It's the laugh that comes when everything hurts, when everything is lost, when all hope is gone and the only power left is a determination to be defiant to the last.

The Coral Sorcerer may have won, but Del will die before he offers him the satisfaction of triumph.

"Before you put me through this fiasco," the Coral Sorcerer tells him. "I was planning to keep you alive. Use you piece by piece as spells required it. But now I see you aren't even worth the trouble. Maybe I'll turn you into a dog, and keep you chained and shivering in the yard until you starve to death. You'd be surprised how many interesting spells call for a dog that's been killed like that. I've wanted to try them for some time."

"I know a joke about a three-legged dog," Del says, feeling more delirious by the moment. He's never been chatty, never been able to banter or make small talk. He's always felt far too shy for that. It's amazing how irrelevant shyness suddenly feels when you've got nothing left to lose. "A few jokes, actually. Want to hear?"

That earns him another kick, this one to his head. Everything goes grey for an endless, meaningless stretch of time, and then Del has to cough again before he chokes on his own blood. He can hear the twins shouting.

Back up to standing again, a ragdoll with no control over himself. Del can't make his eyes focus properly. Everything swims in double, the world a mess.

"Don't. Stop." Kelsie screams. "I'll... I'll play you for him!"

Del turns his head as much as he's able so that he can stare at her in confusion, certain he must have misheard or misunderstood her words.

"You like games, right? Del said that you like games. I... I wager myself and Nicholas. Winner takes all."

"Will you now?" the Coral Sorcerer gives her a sly, thoughtful look. With a wave of his hand, he drops Del down to the ground yet again. "I don't think Addanc and his wife would be pleased to hear that I'd taken all three of the children that belonged to them."

"We don't belong to them," Kelsie says. "We belong to ourselves."

"Not yet you don't. Not until we play for it." The sly look becomes a smirk. "Maybe I'll sell you and your brother back to your mother, once I own you. You'd be worth quite a bit. Certainly more than this half-rate apprentice trash." He kicks one pointed shoe against Del's ribs, hard. "Get up."

Del staggers to his feet swaying as his head swims. "All right," he says. "But when I vomit more blood on your carpet, you can't say you weren't warned."

"You'd really risk yourself and your brother for him?"

the Coral Sorcerer asks with a cruel laugh. "A worthless orphan with nothing more than a young student's knowledge of magic? I could introduce you to magicians a thousand times more valuable. They could teach you tricks you've never dreamed of."

"Of course I would risk myself and my brother for him," Kelsie confirms, her voice barely more than a whisper. "That's what family's supposed to *mean*."

"Fine. And I'll wager the boy and... well, why don't we make it interesting?" The Coral Sorcerer's tone is one of affected boredom. "I wager this whole castle, and all the riches in it. Rowan, a set of scales, please."

Kelsie gasps.

Del blinks, confused for a moment as he realises that the Coral Sorcerer is addressing him. It's not surprising that the man would make him conjure the scales for the game— he clearly enjoys humiliating Del as much as possible in front of the twins, and causing what will doubtlessly be a spectacular nosebleed, given his depleted strength, seems par for that course— but the use of Del's rarely-spoken given name is unexpected.

After a second of thinking about it, Del works out what it's meant to achieve. It's a subtle power play, a way to show Kelsie and Nicholas that the Coral Sorcerer knows things about Del that they don't.

Kelsie is staring at Del in shock. He can almost see the pieces fitting together in her head— the white streak in his hair, his dislike of the story of the lost princess, his childhood spent without home or family beyond servitude to the Warlock.

Del can see the moment when all of that clicks into place.

He wishes he could tell her that no, that's not true. Rowan isn't who he is. Aria isn't who he is. He wants to tell her that they shouldn't fall for it, that it's a trick, that Kelsie and Nicholas know him better than anybody in the world has ever known him, that they're the only two people who have ever looked at him and made him feel like he was *seen*.

But he can see the doubt on Kelsie's face, clear as sunlight across her features, and his heart feels like it's breaking.

He waves his hand and makes the scales appear, just as ordered. When his nose starts bleeding it hardly seems worth the effort to put his cuff against his face to staunch it, since it's surely not the last time he's going to bleed today.

"Since you declared the game, I have right of first round," the Coral Sorcerer says. He goes to the biggest of the desks dotted around the huge room, and pulls out one of the drawers hanging below it, drawing out a roll of sewing tools. The little steel needle which he places on one side of the set of scales gleams, and through its eye Del can see something shifting and moving in the dark.

Kelsie takes a deep breath and says. "All right."

Her counter-move also takes the form of a needle, as she puts down the tiny dart that she'd picked up in their visit to the island ruins, the one she'd said was to help Del remember where they'd been.

Del waves a hand and the scales begin to weigh their two sides against each other, tipping one way and then the other. When they come to a stop it's at a level that's almost, almost even... but ever-so-slightly tilted to Kelsie's side.

"No match!" the Coral Sorcerer gloats. "First round goes to me. Your move, girlie."

Kelsie swallows nervously, her hands shaking ever so slightly as she opens her little pouch and draws out her next playing piece. It's the glass eye that the shopkeeper gave Del. Kelsie places it down on her side of the scales with a click, and when she takes her hand away it rolls to and fro a little before settling in position. The pupil stares at nothing, straight upwards.

The Coral Sorcerer scoffs at the offering. "You'll need to do better than that if you want to stand any chance of winning."

Smirking, he reaches over and plucks the thimble off his work table, placing it on his side of the scales. Del locks the balance and weighs the trinkets, and his heart sinks as the Coral Sorcerer triumphs for a second time as the scales measure the two items as equal.

They are only tiny victories, Del tries to tell himself. *Kelsie could still tip the game in her favour if she can manage to gain a single big advantage.*

But she looks so small, and so very, very scared as she blinks away her tears to see what the Coral Sorcerer's next move is.

It's the inner cogs and workings of a tiny pocket watch, the gears still ticking in perfect time despite no obvious way to wind it up.

Kelsie reaches into her bag again and pulls out a tiny object, too small even to be a baby's tooth. "A crooked bone, from the heart of a rat king," she explains, and sets it on her side of the scales.

The two sides balance perfectly. Kelsie lets out a loud whoosh of breath in relief. Del's thudding heart almost skips a beat.

"Two to one. Good. I was afraid I'd get to three and the game would be over too quickly," the Coral Sorcerer says with a thin smile. "Looks like we're playing best of five, then."

"Best of five," Kelsie agrees.

"I'll even let you have the opening play on both the remaining turns, if you like," the Coral Sorcerer offers. "It's the easier position to play. Let it never be said I'm not a fair competitor."

Del thinks of pointing out that bending the rules like that is, technically, the opposite of being a fair competitor, and that there's no way the Coral Sorcerer is doing it for Kelsie's benefit. But she's already nodding in agreement and reaching into her bag to begin the next round, so Del stays silent.

It's the shard of stained glass that she took from

the church ruins, a tiny jagged thing no bigger than a knucklebone, a gift given to her by a nightmare as a sign of absolution.

The Coral Sorcerer counters with a coin, and as soon as Del sees it he knows the round has gone to Kelsie. The Sorcerer has overestimated the magical weight of the shard, obviously assuming that something so innocuous-looking must be deceptively powerful. But it's only glass, and so the scales wobble before settling on a tilt.

"Two to two," Nicholas says in a subdued voice. "One last round."

Del tries very hard not to hope. It will hurt more if he hopes. His palms are damp.

Kelsie's fingers drift to her throat, playing with the chain of her locket. The Coral Sorcerer's eyes gleam, watching her as avidly as a cat about to pounce upon its prey.

Del's pulse is so fast he feels as if there are birds trying to break out of his ribcage, battering against the bone with all their might as their wings flutter frantically.

He tries to catch Nicholas's eye, hoping that by the strange telepathy the twins share he can convey to Kelsie that she *mustn't play the locket.* If she plays the locket they are lost for certain, because the Coral Sorcerer will have no trouble at all guessing the exact weight of a few bits of hair clipped by a sentimental little girl.

There is no special magic in friendship or love, no twist that would save them if she tried it.

Nicholas looks as blank as he did that night they first came to him at his school. It seems almost impossible to Del that not much time at all has passed since then. It seems like an entire lifetime ago.

Blank, numb, closed off— Nicholas is completely shuttered, unreadable, and won't meet Del's eyes. Del wonders if his own heart is pounding so hard because it is trying to break.

Kelsie shakes her head a little, as if arguing with herself, and drops her hand away from the locket. Del's legs go wobbly with relief and he sags, huffing out a hard breath. It earns him a glare from the Coral Sorcerer, but Del doesn't care. He'll take the smallest piece of hope he can, right now.

His relief is brutally short-lived, however, for a moment later Kelsie reaches into her little suede bag and pulls free a creased playing card, suit-side up. The Jack of Spades.

It takes a second for Del to place the origin of the object. That night on the beach, when they'd played card games by the fire, and in the morning Kelsie had helped him cut his hair.

"T...there," Kelsie stammers, dropping it onto her side of the scales with a shaking hand, giving Del a trembling smile. He tries to return it, but his face feels frozen.

For a moment, the whole world feels frozen. And then the Coral Sorcerer laughs.

It's a gloating, satisfied sound. "You stupid child. A bluff with a playing card? I'm not some gullible idiot taking a gamble with a street busker. You think I've never seen that trick before?"

Kelsie's nervous smile collapses, her face draining to white with fear. "Wait—"

"No. No waiting. You've begun to bore me."

With that the Coral Sorcerer waves a hand, conjuring a single feather out of thin air and dropping it on his side of the scales. "There. Worthlessness for worthlessness. Call the balance, Rowan."

"No, wait, stop," Kelsie begs, her voice trembling as she pleads. The Coral Sorcerer ignores her. Feeling sick to his stomach, Del snaps his fingers to lock the scales in place, so they can weigh up each side and find the winner.

There's no wobbling or uncertainty with the scales this time. Kelsie's side *slams* down, as if she's loaded it up with weights made of lead. The motion is so violent that it throws the Coral Sorcerer's feather up into the air, where it floats back down to its place on the scale and rests, weightless and defeated.

"Del may be nothing but a young student," Kelsie says.

"But have you ever heard what happens to teachers who are foolish enough to hurt the people I love?"

Her whole demeanour has changed. There's no hesitancy to her, no trembles or stammers. She holds her head up high, staring down the Coral Sorcerer, daring him to contest her victory.

"I win. He's mine. Now get out of here. This place is mine and you are not welcome. You are never welcome here again," she tells him, imperious as a queen. "Tell our parents they are not to search for us. We have all the magic of this tower at our disposal, and the quest would not go well for them."

The Coral Sorcerer looks at the three of them with poisonous, predatory hatred in his eyes.

"You arrogant little fool. If you think that I'll—" he starts to say, but before he gets any further Kelsie moves her hand through the air in a sharp slicing motion.

"Go *away*," she snaps, more anger in her voice, more loathing, than Del has ever heard from her.

Kelsie picks up the heavy, jagged rock she'd collected in the passageway, and throws it right at the man's head.

The Coral Sorcerer vanishes with a loud cracking sound, the force of the spell knocking over a table and spilling some books out of their shelves. And then it's just the three of them, Kelsie and Nicholas and Del.

Any huge dramatic reunion this might have led to is delayed, however, when the world around Del suddenly goes grey and slides sideways. As he collapses, he can hear the others shouting, and he wants to answer them but before he can the grey blots out to black and everything goes quiet.

The next thing Del is aware of is waking up in a bed. A proper bed, not a lumpy itchy thing in a freezing attic, or a bedroll on a church ground, or the hollow of a tree. This is a huge, soft, warm bed, and for a moment he feels absolutely sure that he's back at the inn and their adventure is just beginning, and sometime in the night his cold little spot behind the door became too uncomfortable and he climbed up onto the mattress despite his misgivings.

Everything is hazy and quiet, and Del is sure he has never wanted anything as much as he wants to just stay here and rest, and let his aching body and exhausted mind recover from everything that's happened.

That thought prods him into waking up properly. Because he's not at the inn and their journey hasn't just begun. He's battered and bruised and his right forearm is bound up tightly with a sweet-smelling poultice which has drawn all the pain and swollen soreness out of the wound at the end of his wrist where his hand used to be. He opens his eyes.

The glass in the windows is old, bubbled and warped and thick. It makes the moonlight come through more like pale water, strange ripples and distortions and shadows dancing over the walls and ceiling, blue-grey and ghostly.

It paints the bruises and scrapes on Nicholas's face in purple-black, sharpening every one of his freckles to a tiny dark blotch against his skin, his eyelashes like crow feathers. His mouth is half-open as he sleeps and there's a tiny furrow between his eyebrows. Even in dreams, Nicholas can't shrug off his brittle nature, the combative stance he uses to brace against the world.

The other side of the bed is empty, still warm when

Del tests his palm against the pillow. Wherever Kelsie has slipped away to, she hasn't been gone for very long.

Del thinks about getting up, but before he can accomplish more than a sitting position the bedroom door opens and Kelsie slips back inside. The voluminous nightshirt she wears makes her look even smaller and slighter than she already is. When she sees him sitting up, she grins and clambers back onto the bed.

"*You* have been asleep for *two days*," she says accusingly, prodding Del in the breastbone with her index finger.

"I wasn't *asleep*," Del grumbles, batting her hand away. "I was *unconscious*."

"*Unconscious* people don't *snore*," Kelsie replies gleefully.

"I don't *snore*." It seems important, in the face of all they've gone through, for Del to defend whatever dignity he has left. He feels lightheaded, like there's no way that this can possibly the real outcome of it all. It's too... things like this don't happen to him.

"Hey," Kelsie says, softer than her tone a moment earlier. "Del? Is it your arm? I can change the bandage if—"

He blinks to clear his vision, wiping at his cheeks quickly with his remaining hand and giving her a wobbly smile. "No, no. I'm fine."

"It's the *middle of the night*," Nicholas interrupts, flailing out with one hand without opening his eyes to smack whoever's body part is closest. It happens to be Del's knee, and the slap is hard enough to sting a little even through the thick coverlet. "Go back to *sleep*, the both of you."

"I wasn't *asleep*—" Del starts to protest again, but the pillow is so soft under his head as he lies back down again that the rest of his words slip away from him.

There's sunlight outside, the next time Del opens his eyes. There's a fire hissing and popping in the fireplace, and the smell of freshly made toast and tea in the air. If his last waking felt too good to be true, then this is just getting a bit ridiculous. He shuts his eyes again, hoping to make the dream linger for just a few more moments.

"Too late, I saw you, I know you're awake. Get up, lazybones," Nicholas says, from the same direction as the crackles and snaps of the fire. Del risks opening his eyes again, and sitting up in bed.

Nicholas still has the look of someone who has been very ill for some time— his face is gaunt and hollow-eyed, his movements small and careful to preserve as much precious energy as possible. There are two pieces of toast with jam and a cup of tea on the table beside his armchair, and a knitted rug wrapped around his nightshirt-clad shoulders.

"Is there more food?" Del asks. "Where's Kelsie?"

"She went through the trapdoor. There's bread." Nicholas waves a hand at the door to the bedroom. "In the kitchen. There's a toasting fork next to the fire there."

"Come on, give me one of your pieces," Del says, climbing out of bed and walking gingerly over to the other armchair near the fire. He has a bit of a headache, but apart from that feels mostly intact and healing, if tired and a little sore. "I'll go get the bread in a minute when I've woken up, and make you a replacement."

"Shove off. Make your own toast," grumbles Nicholas. "It's not my fault you weren't awake when Kels made this batch."

"Ha! You didn't even make it yourself. Come on, lend a hand." He waves his bandaged wrist.

Nicholas gives Del an utterly nonplussed look. "Did you just... was that... that's the most appalling pun I've ever had the misfortune of hearing. It doesn't even make any *sense*."

Del stands up, leaning across Nicholas and stealing one of the pieces of toast before the other boy can react.

"Mm. Nice jam. What's Kelsie gone to the city for?" Del asks around a mouthful.

"Clothes. There's enough food here, but she got tired

of wearing too-big shirts and rolled-up trousers from the closets. She should be back soon." Nicholas nods to another little table off in the corner of the room. "There's a chess set, if you wanted to have a game."

Chess isn't one of Del's strengths— cards are a chance game more than anything else, and so it didn't matter much that he only had rare opportunities to play. But chess is a game of skill and tactics, and for all that years working under the Ruby Warlock had demanded self-preservation and determined cunning, Del hasn't had much practice in playing a game against an opponent. He sighs and then nods, bracing himself against the eventual defeat.

"Don't sound so enthusiastic," mutters Nicholas sarcastically, rolling his eyes. He pulls the chequer-board-topped table over to the armchairs, and they set up the pieces.

"Kels has gone into the city a few times," he goes on, as they begin the game. "She says that lots of people know who she is, all of a sudden. I guess word's started to get around about what happened. I never thought of magicians and spell-casters as gossips, but apparently they are."

"Your mother and step-father will hear about it soon enough, then." Del keeps his voice as neutral as he can, keeping his eyes on the chess game. "They might come looking. In the city, I mean."

"Yes," Nicholas agrees. "Kels and I have discussed it a lot. It's too likely they'll track us down eventually, if we stay, but she's avoided them so far, and now that you're awake we can start planning properly to leave here. We didn't want to make anything concrete without your input."

Del doesn't know what to feel about that. Or, rather, he feels so many different things that it feels like the wisest course of action to just swallow down the lump in his throat and think about something else. "You said people know who she is, as well as what's happened. They know she defeated a sorcerer?"

Nicholas nods, moving another chess piece as he

answers. "Yes. They've started... they're calling her the Carnelian Witch."

Del can't help the delighted smile that news gives him. "Your mother's going to be furious when she hears."

"People keep talking about the Carnelian Witch and her *consorts*. I'm not sure it's really all that appropriate, calling me her consort when I'm her *brother*."

"So people know it was all three of us?" Del asks. *Us*. What a strange thing for him to say. What a strange thing to sound so easy and right in his mouth, after so many years of having nobody to rely on but himself. "That's a pity. I was planning to claim I did it all *single-handed*."

Nicholas splutters, even more outraged by this pun than by the first. "You're awful. Really awful. Check, by the way."

Del looks down at the board and sighs. "Oh, good." He moves his king out of check, and wonders how many more moves he's got left before he's trapped completely. It's practically inevitable at this point.

"You could... now that we're safe," says Nicholas. "You could change into a girl and back again. That would give you your hand back, wouldn't it?"

Del chews on his lip and keeps his eyes on the black-and-white squares of the board, the little pieces frozen mid-battle across the terrain. "I... I sort of like having it like this," he confesses quietly. "I know it's ugly, but... it's proof. Of the things that happened. I don't mind it."

"You aren't ugly," Nicholas says, familiar annoyance in his voice. "You aren't... you aren't ugly. And I understand. And also, you're in check again."

Del frowns at his little king. "Ugh, yes. Is it just check or is it checkmate? Because I'm st—"

"If you stay 'stumped', I'll thump you," Nicholas cuts him off, only half-teasing. Del tries to look innocent.

"What? I had no intention," he answers blithely. "But I concede the game to you, anyway. I lay down my ar—"

Just as Nicholas punches Del's shoulder— and hard, at

that— Kelsie comes into the room.

"I can't leave you two alone for a *minute*," she complains, dropping several wrapped parcels onto the bed. "Honestly, the luckiest thing that happened to us throughout this whole disaster was that it wasn't me who was snatched on that beach. I can't imagine how useless the pair of you would have been at trying to work together to rescue me."

"What *happened?*" Del asks, unable to wait any longer to find out.

"You ate my toast and I beat you at chess," Nicholas answers.

Del ignores him.

Kelsie shrugs. "We won."

"But *how*? What did you do?"

She reaches into the little suede pouch, hanging from the sash of a very pretty new dress.

"Here." She hands him the card. It looks just as it did on the scales, an ordinary Jack of Spades with a crease from where Nicholas put his hand down skewed in a game of Snap.

Now that he's holding it, Del can feel the immense power, the thrum of strong, deep magic embedded in the thin card, connecting it to the invisible net of energy hanging delicately in all the world around them.

Puzzled, he turns it over. On the back of the playing card is a smear of dried blood.

"When I shoved everything into my bag on the beach, the card was squashed up against that handkerchief I loaned you," Kelsie explains. "Some of the blood from your nose must have still been wet. I noticed it later, when we were in the city.

"I didn't know if it would work, not for certain, but... you said blood magic was the most powerful kind, if the blood was given freely. And you cast all of those spells to help me and to help Nicky, so I... I just trusted to hope, I suppose."

"But you seemed so scared..."

Kelsie laughs. "Oh, I was plenty scared. Believe me. But not as scared as I looked, no. I knew that, even after all we've gone through, you still don't think that you know me. You'd think I really was that frightened.

"Your reactions would be genuine, and that they'd make the Coral Sorcerer cocky. It's like we talked about, back at my school. Ego always gets them in the end.

"But now there's no excuse," Kelsie goes on. "No more tricks and secret plans. We have to believe who we are and trust each other with it. All of it."

"If this is about—" Del starts to say, before Kelsie interrupts him, just as he knew she was going to.

"Of course it's about that. You're the rightful hei—"

"No. I'm a runaway skivvy who doesn't feel like I'm a girl *or* a boy. Who only has one hand and isn't any good at chess. Can you imagine how dismayed all those mothers who called their babies Octavia would be, if I came back? I'm hardly the fairytale prince-princess they wanted, am I?"

"Nobody who doesn't know what being poor is like should ever be in charge of lots of money or people, that's what I think," insists Kelsie.

"Double negatives aren't very good grammar," Nicholas teases his sister gently. "Come on, Kels. If he's earned the right to be the rightful anything, it's to just be Del if that's what he wants."

"But..." Kelsie starts, before giving up with a huff of annoyance. "I'm going to try on my new dresses. You're as bad as each other."

Nicholas rolls his eyes. Del gives him a crooked grin, a silent shared laugh over Kelsie's melodrama.

Later, as the two of them explore a little bit of the castle, Del finally has a chance to ask Nicholas something that's been bothering him.

"I was thinking about what Kelsie said earlier, about what if it had been the two of us trying to save her. And...

"It seemed like you... like you jumped in front of me. On the beach."

“Well, yes,” Nicholas admits. “Because... well, I already knew for certain that you and Kelsie would come and find me, if I was in trouble. But I didn’t know if Kelsie and I could manage to save you if we were the ones left behind. It just made for me to do it that way.”

Del doesn’t know what to say to that. “We can’t stay here, you know. Someone’s going to come for us, sooner or later. We’re never going to stop running.”

“Always the pessimist,” Nicholas retorts. “Think of all the places we might go, instead of dwelling on the depressing part of it. I want to get my boat back and fixed, for a start. Oh, here, come look at this carriage. Kelsie found it the first day.”

Kelsie’s already inside the carriage when Del and Nicholas climb up to join her. The windowless exterior’s no bigger than an ordinary city carriage, but the inside is larger than the bedroom where Del woke up, with brightly luminescent white stones inlaid at wainscot-height on the walls to make up for the lack of windows.

It’s an airy, cheerful space, with a set of enamel mugs and a matching kettle hanging from nails in one corner and jars of dried fruit and salted meat and spices and bottles of water all held in place by travel racks on the shelves. There’s an armchair with a stack of books beside it and a writing desk with a stool and a bed almost as wide as the one upstairs.

“This is the sort of thing a magician with real power can do,” Del says, looking around and feeling impressed and embarrassed all at once. “So you see, really, the things I did were always just parlour tricks.”

“Mm,” Kelsie says. She takes his hand in hers and squeezes. “I’ve had enough of magicians with real power, I think. Parlour tricks will do me for a while.”

She looks around the room, a thoughtful expression on her face. “Still, since this is here already, we might as well make use of it.”

“For a while, anyway,” Nicholas agrees. “Though I

wouldn't mind another night or two sleeping out on beaches. I'm sure it's actually rather nice to do so, when it's not such a grim necessity."

The twins' enthusiasm makes Del feel hesitant, almost frightened. He's still not used to only having one hand, still clumsy at ordinary everyday tasks. And now that Kelsie's beginning to come into her own as a magic user, they don't really need him for anything.

"Hey," Kelsie says, as if she can hear his worried thoughts. She bumps his shoulder with her own. "Don't be stupid."

"I'm not sure he can help it," Nicholas offers helpfully.

"We risked a lot for you," Kelsie goes on gravely. "Come on. Risk a little for us."

"You're much easier to beat at chess than Kelsie is. You're practically indispensable."

Del smiles, still unused to the teasing, unsure how long he can make himself trust in his right to be there beside them on their adventures. It might be that all this turns out to be a very bad idea.

But it might be that it all turns out all right, too.

"All right," Del agrees, and smiles at them. "Let's go."

About the Author

Mary Borsellino is an Australian writer in her thirties. She has a bunch of tattoos and a tendency to get passionately involved with things she believes in and loves. Her day job is as a Media Coordinator in the nonprofit sector. Her website is http://maryborsellino.com.

www.ingramcontent.com/pod-product-compliance
Lightning Source LLC
Chambersburg PA
CBHW020614310726
48979CB00008B/1487/J

* 9 7 8 0 6 1 5 7 9 0 8 6 2 *